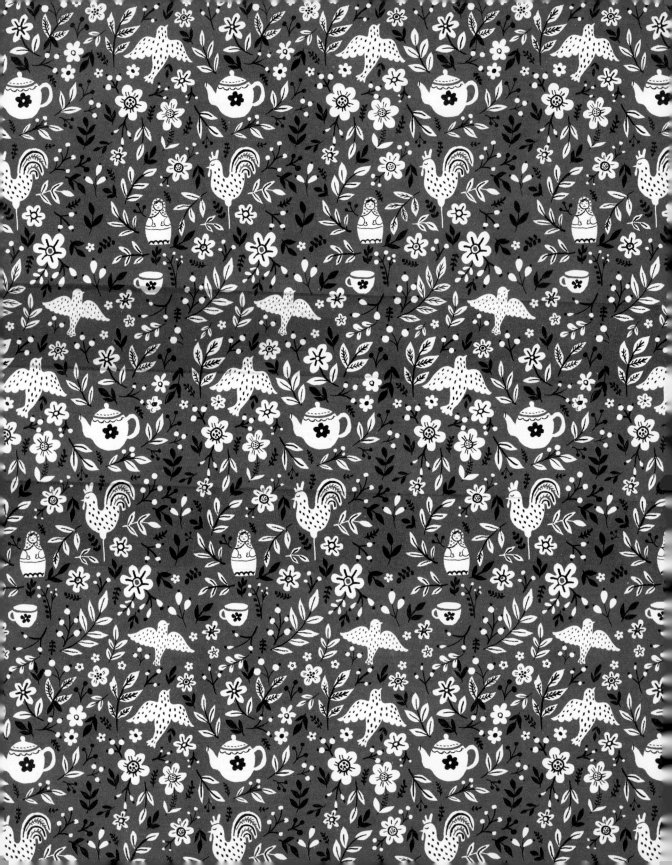

# Russian Tales

# RUSSIAN TALES

## Traditional Stories of Quests and Enchantments

Illustrations by
*Dinara Mirtalipova*

CHRONICLE BOOKS
SAN FRANCISCO

Illustrations by Dinara Mirtalipova, copyright © 2021 by Chronicle Books LLC.

Library of Congress Cataloging-in-Publication Data

Names: Mirtalipova, Dinara, illustrator.
Title: Russian tales : traditional stories of quests and enchantments / illustrations by Dinara Mirtalipova.
Description: San Francisco : Chronicle Books, [2021] | Includes bibliographical references. |
Summary: "An illustrated collection oftraditional Russian folktales"-- Provided by publisher. Identifiers: LCCN 2021000823 (print) | LCCN 2021000824 (ebook) | ISBN 9781797209692 (Hardcover) | ISBN 9781797214788 (eBook) Subjects: LCSH: Tales--Russia (Federation) Classification: LCC GR203.17 .R864 2021  (print) | LCC GR203.17  (ebook) |DDC 392.20947--dc23 LC record available at https://lccn.loc.gov/2021000823 LC ebook record available at https://lccn.loc.gov/2021000824

Manufactured in China.

Design by Maggie Edelman.

10 9 8 7 6 5 4 3

Chronicle books and gifts are available at special quantity discounts to corporations, professional associations, literacy programs, and other organizations. For details and discount information, please contact our premiums department at corporatesales@chroniclebooks.com or at 1-800-759-0190.

Chronicle Books LLC
680 Second Street
San Francisco, California 94107
www.chroniclebooks.com

"Then the Tsarévna threw the net into the deep; fished the King's son up,
took him home, and told her father the whole story."

LEONARD A. MAGNUS,
"The Tsarévich and Dyád'ka"

# Contents

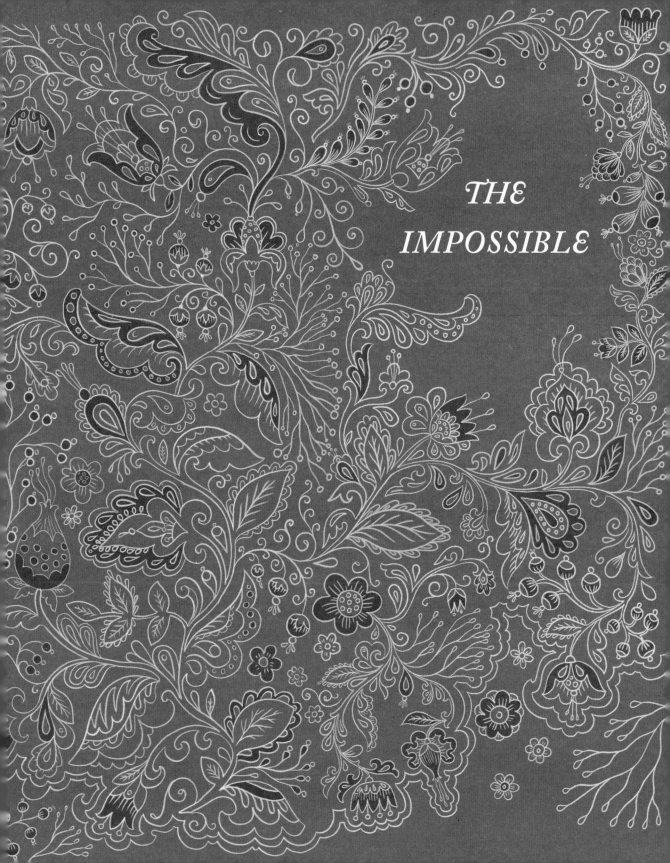

THE
IMPOSSIBLE

# MARYA MOREVNA

In a certain kingdom there lived a Prince Ivan. He had three sisters. The first was the Princess Marya, the second the Princess Olga, the third the Princess Anna. When their father and mother lay at the point of death, they had thus enjoined their son:—"Give your sisters in marriage to the very first suitors who come to woo them. Don't go keeping them by you!"

They died and the Prince buried them, and then, to solace his grief, he went with his sisters into the garden green to stroll. Suddenly the sky was covered by a black cloud; a terrible storm arose.

"Let us go home, sisters!" he cried.

Hardly had they got into the palace, when the thunder pealed, the ceiling split open, and into the room where they were, came flying a falcon bright. The Falcon smote upon the ground, became a brave youth, and said:

"Hail, Prince Ivan! Before I came as a guest, but now I have come as a wooer! I wish to propose for your sister, the Princess Marya."

"If you find favor in the eyes of my sister, I will not interfere with her wishes. Let her marry you in God's name!"

The Princess Marya gave her consent; the Falcon married her and bore her away into his own realm.

Days follow days, hours chase hours; a whole year goes by. One day Prince Ivan and his two sisters went out to stroll in the garden green. Again there arose a stormcloud with whirlwind and lightning.

"Let us go home, sisters!" cried the Prince. Scarcely had they entered the palace, when the thunder crashed, the roof burst into a blaze, the ceiling split in twain, and in flew an eagle. The Eagle smote upon the ground and became a brave youth.

"Hail, Prince Ivan! Before I came as a guest, but now I have come as a wooer!"

And he asked for the hand of the Princess Olga. Prince Ivan replied:

"If you find favor in the eyes of the Princess Olga, then let her marry you. I will not interfere with her liberty of choice."

The Princess Olga gave her consent and married the Eagle. The Eagle took her and carried her off to his own kingdom.

Another year went by. Prince Ivan said to his youngest sister:

"Let us go out and stroll in the garden green!"

They strolled about for a time. Again there arose a stormcloud, with whirlwind and lightning.

"Let us return home, sister!" said he.

They returned home, but they hadn't had time to sit down when the thunder crashed, the ceiling split open, and in flew a raven. The Raven smote upon the floor and became a brave youth. The former youths had been handsome, but this one was handsomer still.

"Well, Prince Ivan! Before I came as a guest, but now I have come as a wooer. Give me the Princess Anna to wife."

"I won't interfere with my sister's freedom. If you gain her affections, let her marry you."

So the Princess Anna married the Raven, and he bore her away to his own realm. Prince Ivan was left alone. A whole year he lived without his sisters; then he grew weary, and said:—

"I will set out in search of my sisters."

He got ready for the journey, he rode and rode, and one day he saw a whole army lying dead on the plain. He cried aloud, "If there be a living man there, let him make answer! who has slain this mighty host?"

There replied unto him a living man:

"All this mighty host has been slain by the fair Princess Marya Morevna."

Prince Ivan rode further on, and came to a white tent, and forth came to meet him the fair Princess Marya Morevna.

"Hail Prince!" says she, "whither does God send you? and is it of your free will or against your will?"

Prince Ivan replied, "Not against their will do brave youths ride!"

"Well, if your business be not pressing, tarry awhile in my tent."

Thereat was Prince Ivan glad. He spent two nights in the tent, and he found favor in the eyes of Marya Morevna, and she married him. The fair Princess, Marya Morevna, carried him off into her own realm.

They spent some time together, and then the Princess took it into her head to go a warring. So she handed over all the housekeeping affairs to Prince Ivan, and gave him these instructions:

"Go about everywhere, keep watch over everything, only do not venture to look into that closet there."

He couldn't help doing so. The moment Marya Morevna had gone he rushed to the closet, pulled open the door, and looked in—there hung Koshchei the Deathless, fettered by twelve chains. Then Koshchei entreated Prince Ivan, saying,—

"Have pity upon me and give me to drink! Ten years long have I been here in torment, neither eating or drinking; my throat is utterly dried up."

The Prince gave him a bucketful of water; he drank it up and asked for more, saying:

"A single bucket of water will not quench my thirst; give me more!"

The Prince gave him a second bucketful. Koshchei drank it up and asked for a third, and when he had swallowed the third bucketful, he regained his former strength, gave his chains a shake, and broke all twelve at once.

"Thanks, Prince Ivan!" cried Koshchei the deathless, "now you will sooner see your own ears than Marya Morevna!" and out of the window he flew in the shape of a terrible whirlwind. And he came up with the fair Princess Marya Morevna as she was going her way, laid hold of her, and carried her off home with him. But Prince Ivan wept full sore, and he arrayed himself and set out a wandering, saying to himself: "Whatever happens, I will go and look for Marya Morevna!"

One day passed, another day passed: at the dawn of the third day he saw a wondrous palace, and by the side of the palace stood an oak, and on the oak sat a falcon bright. Down flew the Falcon from the oak, smote upon the ground, turned into a brave youth and cried aloud:

"Ha, dear brother-in-law! how deals the Lord with you?"

Out came running the Princess Marya, joyfully greeted her brother Ivan, and began enquiring after his health, and telling him all about herself. The Prince spent three days with them, then he said:

"I cannot abide with you; I must go in search of my wife the fair Princess Marya Morevna."

"Hard will it be for you to find her," answered the Falcon. "At all events leave with us your silver spoon. We will look at it and remember you." So Prince Ivan left his silver spoon at the Falcon's, and went on his way again.

On he went one day, on he went another day, and by the dawn of the third day he saw a palace still grander than the former one, and hard by the palace stood an oak, and on the oak sat an eagle. Down flew the eagle from the oak, smote upon the ground, turned into a brave youth, and cried aloud:

"Rise up, Princess Olga! Hither comes our brother dear!"

The Princess Olga immediately ran to meet him, and began kissing him and embracing him, asking after his health and telling him all about herself. With them Prince Ivan stopped three days; then he said:

"I cannot stay here any longer. I am going to look for my wife, the fair Princess Marya Morevna."

"Hard will it be for you to find her," replied the Eagle, "Leave with us a silver fork. We will look at it and remember you."

He left a silver fork behind, and went his way. He travelled one day, he travelled two days; at daybreak on the third day he saw a palace grander than the first two, and near the palace stood an oak, and on the oak sat a raven. Down flew the Raven from the oak, smote upon the ground, turned into a brave youth, and cried aloud:

"Princess Anna, come forth quickly! our brother is coming!"

Out ran the Princess Anna, greeted him joyfully, and began kissing and embracing him, asking after his health and telling him all about herself. Prince Ivan stayed with them three days; then he said:

"Farewell! I am going to look for my wife, the fair Princess Marya Morevna."

"Hard will it be for you to find her," replied the Raven, "Anyhow, leave your silver snuff-box with us. We will look at it and remember you."

The Prince handed over his silver snuff-box, took his leave and went his way. One day he went, another day he went, and on the third day he came to where Marya Morevna was. She caught sight of her love, flung her arms around his neck, burst into tears, and exclaimed:

"Oh, Prince Ivan! why did you disobey me, and go looking into the closet and letting out Koshchei the Deathless?"

"Forgive me, Marya Morevna! Remember not the past; much better fly with me while Koshchei the Deathless is out of sight. Perhaps he won't catch us."

So they got ready and fled. Now Koshchei was out hunting. Towards evening he was returning home, when his good steed stumbled beneath him.

"Why stumblest thou, sorry jade? scentest thou some ill?"

The steed replied:

"Prince Ivan has come and carried off Marya Morevna."

"Is it possible to catch them?"

"It is possible to sow wheat, to wait till it grows up, to reap it and thresh it, to grind it to flour, to make five pies of it, to eat those pies, and then to start in pursuit—and even then to be in time."

Koshchei galloped off and caught up Prince Ivan.

"Now," says he, "this time I will forgive you, in return for your kindness in giving me water to drink. And a second time I will forgive you; but the third time beware! I will cut you to bits."

Then he took Marya Morevna from him, and carried her off. But Prince Ivan sat down on a stone and burst into tears. He wept and wept—and then returned back again to Marya Morevna. Now Koshchei the Deathless happened not to be at home.

"Let us fly, Marya Morevna!"

"Ah, Prince Ivan! he will catch us."

"Suppose he does catch us. At all events we shall have spent an hour or two together."

So they got ready and fled. As Koshchei the Deathless was returning home, his good steed stumbled beneath him.

"Why stumblest thou, sorry jade? scentest thou some ill?"

"Prince Ivan has come and carried off Marya Morevna."

"Is it possible to catch them?"

"It is possible to sow barley, to wait till it grows up, to reap it and thresh it, to brew beer, to drink ourselves drunk on it, to sleep our fill, and then to set off in pursuit—and yet to be in time."

Koshchei galloped off, caught up Prince Ivan:

"Didn't I tell you that you should not see Marya Morevna any more than your own ears?"

And he took her away and carried her off home with him.

Prince Ivan was left there alone. He wept and wept; then he went back again after Marya Morevna. Koshchei happened to be away from home at that moment.

"Let us fly, Marya Morevna."

"Ah, Prince Ivan! He is sure to catch us and hew you in pieces."

"Let him hew away! I cannot live without you."

So they got ready and fled.

Koshchei the Deathless was returning home when his good steed stumbled beneath him.

"Why stumblest thou? scentest thou any ill?"

"Prince Ivan has come and has carried off Marya Morevna."

Koshchei galloped off, caught Prince Ivan, chopped him into little pieces, put them in a barrel, smeared it with pitch and bound it with iron hoops, and flung it into the blue sea. But Marya Morevna he carried off home.

At that very time, the silver turned black which Prince Ivan had left with his brothers-in-law.

"Ah!" said they, "the evil is accomplished sure enough!"

Then the Eagle hurried to the blue sea, caught hold of the barrel, and dragged it ashore; the Falcon flew away for the Water of Life, and the Raven for the Water of Death.

Afterwards they all three met, broke open the barrel, took out the remains of Prince Ivan, washed them, and put them together in fitting order. The Raven sprinkled them with the Water of Death—the pieces joined together, the body became whole. The Falcon sprinkled it with the Water of Life—Prince Ivan shuddered, stood up, and said:

"Ah! what a time I've been sleeping!"

"You'd have gone on sleeping a good deal longer, if it hadn't been for us," replied his brothers-in-law. "Now come and pay us a visit."

"Not so, brothers; I shall go and look for Marya Morevna."

And when he had found her, he said to her:

"Find out from Koshchei the Deathless whence he got so good a steed."

So Marya Morevna chose a favorable moment, and began asking Koshchei about it. Koshchei replied:

"Beyond thrice nine lands, in the thirtieth kingdom, on the other side of the fiery river, there lives a Baba Yaga. She has so good a mare that she flies right round the world on it every day. And she has many other splendid mares. I watched her herds for three days without losing a single mare, and in return for that the Baba Yaga gave me a foal."

"But how did you get across the fiery river?"

"Why, I've a handkerchief of this kind—when I wave it thrice on the right hand, there springs up a very lofty bridge and the fire cannot reach it."

Marya Morevna listened to all this, and repeated it to Prince Ivan, and she carried off the handkerchief and gave it to him. So he managed to get across the fiery river, and then went on to the Baba Yaga's. Long went he on without getting anything either to eat or to drink. At last he came across an outlandish bird and its young ones. Says Prince Ivan:

"I'll eat one of these chickens."

"Don't eat it, Prince Ivan!" begs the outlandish bird; "some time or other I'll do you a good turn."

He went on farther and saw a hive of bees in the forest.

"I'll get a bit of honeycomb," says he.

"Don't disturb my honey, Prince Ivan!" exclaims the queen bee; "some time or other I'll do you a good turn."

So he didn't disturb it, but went on. Presently there met him a lioness with her cub.

"Anyhow I'll eat this lion cub," says he; "I'm so hungry, I feel quite unwell!"

"Please let us alone, Prince Ivan" begs the lioness; "some time or other I'll do you a good turn."

"Very well; have it your own way," says he.

Hungry and faint he wandered on, walked farther and farther and at last came to where stood the house of the Baba Yaga. Round the house were set twelve poles in a circle, and on each of eleven of these poles was stuck a human head, the twelfth alone remained unoccupied.

"Hail, granny!"

"Hail, Prince Ivan! wherefore have you come? Is it of your own accord, or on compulsion?"

"I have come to earn from you a heroic steed."

"So be it, Prince, you won't have to serve a year with me, but just three days. If you take good care of my mares, I'll give you a heroic steed. But if you don't—why then you mustn't be annoyed at finding your head stuck on top of the last pole up there."

Prince Ivan agreed to these terms. The Baba Yaga gave him food and drink, and bid him set about his business. But the moment he had driven the mares afield, they cocked up their tails, and away they tore across the meadows in all directions. Before the Prince had time to look round, they were all out of sight. Thereupon he began to weep and to disquiet himself, and then he sat down upon a stone and went to sleep. But when the sun was near its setting, the outlandish bird came flying up to him, and awakened him saying:—

"Arise, Prince Ivan! the mares are at home now."

The Prince arose and returned home. There the Baba Yaga was storming and raging at her mares, and shrieking:—

"Whatever did ye come home for?"

"How could we help coming home?" said they. "There came flying birds from every part of the world, and all but pecked our eyes out."

"Well, well! to-morrow don't go galloping over the meadows, but disperse amid the thick forests."

Prince Ivan slept all night. In the morning the Baba Yaga says to him:—

"Mind, Prince! if you don't take good care of the mares, if you lose merely one of them—your bold head will be stuck on that pole!"

He drove the mares afield. Immediately they cocked up their tails and dispersed among the thick forests. Again did the Prince sit down on the stone, weep and weep, and then go to sleep. The sun went down behind the forest. Up came running the lioness.

"Arise, Prince Ivan! The mares are all collected."

Prince Ivan arose and went home. More than ever did the Baba Yaga storm at her mares and shriek:—

"Whatever did ye come back home for?"

"How could we help coming back? Beasts of prey came running at us from all parts of the world, all but tore us utterly to pieces."

"Well, to-morrow run off into the blue sea."

Again did Prince Ivan sleep through the night. Next morning the Baba Yaga sent him forth to watch the mares:

"If you don't take good care of them," says she, "your bold head will be stuck on that pole!"

He drove the mares afield. Immediately they cocked up their tails, disappeared from sight, and fled into the blue sea. There they stood, up to their necks in water. Prince Ivan sat down on the stone, wept, and fell asleep. But when the sun had set behind the forest, up came flying a bee and said:—

"Arise, Prince! The mares are all collected. But when you get home, don't let the Baba Yaga set eyes on you, but go into the stable and hide behind the mangers. There you will find a sorry colt rolling in the muck. Do you steal it, and at the dead of night ride away from the house."

Prince Ivan arose, slipped into the stable, and lay down behind the mangers, while the Baba Yaga was storming away at her mares and shrieking:—

"Why did ye come back?"

"How could we help coming back? There came flying bees in countless numbers from all parts of the world, and began stinging us on all sides till the blood came!"

The Baba Yaga went to sleep. In the dead of the night Prince Ivan stole the sorry colt, saddled it, jumped on its back, and galloped away to the fiery river. When he came to that river he waved the handkerchief three times on the right hand, and suddenly, springing goodness knows whence, there hung across the river, high in the air, a splendid bridge. The Prince rode across the bridge and waved the handkerchief twice only on the left hand; there remained across the river a thin—ever so thin a bridge!

When the Baba Yaga got up in the morning, the sorry colt was not to be seen! Off she set in pursuit. At full speed did she fly in her iron mortar, urging it on with the pestle, sweeping away her traces with the broom. She dashed up to the fiery river, gave a glance, and said, "A capital bridge!" She drove on to the bridge, but had only got half-way when the bridge broke in two, and the Baba Yaga went flop into the river. There truly did she meet with a cruel death!

Prince Ivan fattened up the colt in the green meadows, and it turned into a wondrous steed. Then he rode to where Marya Morevna was. She came running out, and flung herself on his neck, crying:—

"By what means has God brought you back to life?"

"Thus and thus," says he. "Now come along with me."

"I am afraid, Prince Ivan! If Koshchei catches us, you will be cut in pieces again."

"No, he won't catch us! I have a splendid heroic steed now; it flies just like a bird." So they got on its back and rode away.

Koshchei the Deathless was returning home when his horse stumbled beneath him.

"What art thou stumbling for, sorry jade? dost thou scent any ill?"

"Prince Ivan has come and carried off Marya Morevna."

"Can we catch them?"

"God knows! Prince Ivan has a horse now which is better than I."

"Well, I can't stand it," says Koshchei the Deathless. "I will pursue."

After a time he came up with Prince Ivan, lighted on the ground, and was going to chop him up with his sharp sword. But at that moment Prince Ivan's horse smote Koshchei the Deathless full swing with its hoof, and cracked his skull, and the Prince made an end of him with a club. Afterwards the Prince heaped up a pile of wood, set fire to it, burnt Koshchei the Deathless on the pyre, and scattered his ashes to the wind. Then Marya Morevna mounted Koshchei's horse and Prince Ivan got on his own, and they rode away to visit first the Raven, and then the Eagle, and then the Falcon. Wherever they went they met with a joyful greeting.

"Ah, Prince Ivan! why, we never expected to see you again. Well, it wasn't for nothing that you gave yourself so much trouble. Such a beauty as Marya Morevna one might search for all the world over—and never find one like her!"

And so they visited, and they feasted; and afterwards they went off to their own realm.

# IVAN the PEASANT'S SON and the LITTLE MAN HIMSELF ONE-FINGER TALL, HIS MUSTACHE SEVEN VERSTS in LENGTH

In a certain kingdom in a certain land there lived a Tsar, and in the courtyard of the Tsar was a pillar, and in the pillar three rings, one gold, one silver, and the third copper. One night the Tsar dreamed that there was a horse tied to the gold ring, that every hair on him was silver, and the clear moon was on his forehead. In the morning the Tsar rose up and ordered it to be proclaimed that whoever could interpret the dream and get the horse for him, to that man would he give his daughter, and one half the kingdom in addition.

At the summons of the Tsar a multitude of princes, *boyárs*, and all kinds of lords assembled. No man could explain the dream; no man would undertake to get the horse. At last they explained to the Tsar that such and such a poor man had a son Ivan, who could interpret the dream and get the horse.

The Tsar commanded them to summon Ivan. They summoned him. The Tsar asked, "Canst thou explain my dream and get the horse?"

"Tell me first," answered Ivan, "what the dream was, and what horse thou dost need."

The Tsar said: "Last night I dreamed that a horse was tied to the gold ring in my courtyard; every hair on him was silver, and on his forehead the clear moon."

"That is not a dream, but a reality; for last night the twelve-headed serpent came to thee on that horse and wanted to steal thy daughter."

"Is it possible to get that horse?"

"It is," answered Ivan; "but only when my fifteenth year is passed."

Ivan was then but twelve years old. The Tsar took him to his court, gave him food and drink till his fifteenth year.

When his fifteenth year had passed, Ivan said to the Tsar: "Now give me a horse on which I can ride to the place where the serpent is."

The Tsar led him to his stables and showed him all his horses; but he could not find a single one, by reason of his strength and weight. When he placed his hero's hand on any horse, that horse fell to the ground; and he said to the Tsar: "Let me go to the open country to seek a horse of sufficient strength."

The Tsar let him go. Ivan the peasant's son looked for three years; nowhere could he find a horse. He was returning to the Tsar in tears, when an old man happened to meet him, and asked, "Why dost thou weep, young man?"

To this question Ivan answered rudely; just chased the old man away.

The old man said: "Look out, young fellow; do not speak ill."

Ivan went away a little from the old man, and thought, "Why have I offended the old man? Old people know much."

He returned, caught up with the old man, fell down before him, and said: "Grandfather, forgive me! I offended thee through grief. This is what I am crying about: three years have I travelled through the open country among many herds; nowhere can I find a horse to suit me."

The old man said: "Go to such a village; there in the stable of a poor peasant is a mare; that mare has a mangy colt; take the colt and feed him,—he will be strong enough for thee."

Ivan bowed down to the old man, and went to the village; went straight to the peasant's stable; saw the mare with the mangy colt, on which he put his hands. The colt did not quiver in the least. Ivan took him from the peasant, fed him some time, came to the Tsar, and said that he had a horse. Then he began to make ready to visit the serpent.

The Tsar asked: "How many men dost thou need, Ivan?"

"I need no men," replied Ivan; "I can get the horse alone. Thou mightest give me perhaps half a dozen to send on messages."

The Tsar gave him six men; they made ready and set out. Whether they travelled long or short it is unknown to any man; only this is known,—that they came to a fiery river. Over the river was a bridge; near the river an enormous forest. In that forest they pitched a tent, got many things to drink, and began to eat and make merry.

Ivan the peasant's son said to his comrades: "Let us stand guard every night in turn, and see if any man passes the river."

It happened that when any of Ivan's comrades went on guard, each one of them got drunk in the evening and could see nothing. At last Ivan himself went on guard; and just at midnight he saw that a three-headed serpent was crossing the river, and the serpent called, "I have no enemy, no calumniator, unless one enemy and one calumniator, Ivan the peasant's son; but the raven hasn't brought his bones in a bladder yet."

Ivan the peasant's son sprang from under the bridge. "Thou liest; I am here!"

"If thou art here, then let us make trial;" and the serpent on horseback advanced against Ivan. But Ivan went forth on foot, gave a blow with his sabre, and cut off the three heads of the serpent, took the horse for himself, and tied him to the tent.

The next night Ivan the peasant's son killed the six-headed serpent, the third night the nine-headed one, and threw them into the fiery river. When he went on guard the fourth night the twelve-headed serpent came, and began to speak wrathfully. "Who art thou, Ivan the peasant's son? Come out this minute to me! Why didst thou kill my sons?"

Ivan the peasant's son slipped out and said: "Let me go first to my tent, and then I will fight with thee."

"Well, go on."

Ivan ran to his comrades. "Here, boys, is a bowl, look into it; when it shall be filled with blood, come to me."

He returned and stood against the serpent; they rushed and struck each other. Ivan at the first blow cut four heads off the serpent, but went himself to his knees in the earth; when they met the second time, Ivan cut three heads off and sank to his waist in the earth; the third time they met he cut off three more heads, and sank to his breast in the earth; at last he cut off one head, and sank to his neck in the earth. Then only did his comrades think of him; they looked, and saw that the blood was running over the edge of the bowl. They hastened out, cut off the last head of the serpent, and pulled Ivan out of the earth. Ivan took the serpent's horse and led him to the tent.

Night passed, morning came; the good youth began to eat, drink, and be merry. Ivan the peasant's son rose up from the merry-making and said to his comrades, "Do ye wait here." He turned into a cat, and went along the bridge over the fiery river, came to the house where the serpents used to live, and began to make friends with the cats there. In the house there remained alive only the old mother of the serpents and her three daughters-in-law; they were sitting in the chamber talking to one another. "How could we destroy that scoundrel, that Ivan the peasant's son?"

The youngest daughter-in-law said: "I'll bring hunger on the road, and turn myself into an apple-tree, so that when he eats an apple it will tear him to pieces in a moment."

The second daughter-in-law said: "I will bring thirst on the road, and turn myself into a well; let him try to drink."

The eldest said: "I'll bring sleep and make a bed of myself; let Ivan try to lie down, he'll die in a minute."

At last the old woman said: "I'll open my mouth from earth to sky and swallow them all."

Ivan heard what they said, went out of the chamber, turned into a man, and went back to his comrades. "Now, boys, make ready for the road."

They made ready, went their way, and to begin with a terrible hunger appeared on the road, so that they had nothing to eat. They saw an apple-tree. Ivan's comrades wanted to pluck the apples, but Ivan would not let them. "That is not an apple-tree," said he; and began to slash at it: blood came out. Another time thirst came upon them. Ivan saw a well; he would not let them drink from it; he began to slash at it: blood came forth. Then sleep came on them; there was a bed on the road. Ivan cut it to pieces. They came to the jaws stretched from the earth to the sky. What was to be done? They thought of jumping through on a run. No man was able to jump through save Ivan; and he was borne out of the trouble by his wonderful steed, every hair of which was silver, and the bright moon on his forehead.

He came to a river; at the river was a hut; there he was met by a little man, himself one finger tall, his mustache seven versts in length, who said: "Give me the horse; and if thou wilt not give him quietly, I'll take him by force."

Ivan answered: "Leave me, cursed reptile, or I'll crush thee under the horse."

The little man himself, one finger tall, his mustache seven versts in length, knocked him on to the ground, sat on the horse, and rode away. Ivan went into the hut and grieved greatly for his horse. In the hut was lying on the stove a footless, handless man, and he said to Ivan: "Listen, good hero,—I know not how to call thee by name. Why didst thou try to fight with him? I was something more of a hero than thou, and still he gnawed my hands and feet off."

"Why?"

"Because I ate bread on his table."

Ivan began to ask how he could win his horse back. The footless, handless said,—

"Go to such a river and take the ferry, ferry for three years, take money from no man: then thou mayest win the horse back."

Ivan bowed down to him, went to the river, took the ferry, and ferried three whole years for nothing. Once it happened to him to ferry over three old men; they offered him money, he would not take it.

"Tell me, good hero, why thou takest no money?"

He said, "According to a promise."

"What promise?"

"A malicious man took my horse, and good people told me to take the ferry for three years, and receive money from no man."

The old men said: "If thou choosest, Ivan, we are ready to help thee to get back thy horse."

"Help me, my friends."

The old men were not common people; they were the Freezer, the Devourer, and the Wizard. The Wizard went out on the shore, made the picture of a boat in the sand and said: "Well, brothers, you see this boat?"

"We see it."

"Sit in it."

All four sat in the boat.

The Wizard said: "Now, light little boat, do me a service as thou didst do before."

Straightway the boat rose in the air, and in a flash, just like an arrow sent from a bow, it brought them to a great stony mountain. At that mountain stood a house, and in the house lived the little man,—himself one finger tall, his mustache seven versts in length. The old men sent Ivan to ask for the horse. Ivan began to ask.

The little man said: "Steal the Tsar's daughter and bring her to me; then I'll give thee the horse."

Ivan told this to his comrades. They left him at once and went to the Tsar. The Tsar knew what they had come for, and commanded his servants to heat the bath red hot. "Let them suffocate there," said he. Then he asked his guests to the bath. They thanked him and went. The Wizard commanded the Freezer to go first. The Freezer went into the bath and made it cool. Then they washed and steamed themselves, and came to the Tsar. He ordered a great dinner to be given, and a multitude of all kinds of food was on the table. The Devourer began and ate everything. In the night they came together, stole the Tsar's daughter, and brought her to the little man himself, one finger tall, his mustache seven versts in length. They gave him the Tsar's daughter and got the horse.

Ivan bowed down to the old men, sat on the horse, and went to the Tsar. He travelled and travelled, stopped in an open field to rest, put up his tent, and lay down. He woke up, threw out his hand, the Tsar's daughter was by him; he was delighted, and asked, "How didst thou come here?"

"I turned into a pin, and stuck myself into thy collar."

That moment she turned into a pin again. Ivan stuck her into his collar and travelled on; came to the Tsar. The Tsar saw the wondrous horse, received the good hero with honor, and told how his daughter had been stolen.

Ivan said: "Do not grieve, I have brought her back."

He went into the next chamber; the Tsarevna turned into a fair maiden. Ivan took her by the hand and brought her to the Tsar.

The Tsar was still more rejoiced. He took the horse for himself, and gave his daughter to Ivan. Ivan is living yet with his young wife.

# THE SMITH and the DEMON

Once upon a time there was a Smith, and he had one son, a sharp, smart, six-year-old boy. One day the old man went to church, and as he stood before a picture of the Last Judgment he saw a Demon painted there—such a terrible one!—black, with horns and a tail.

"O my!" says he to himself. "Suppose I get just such another painted for the smithy." So he hired an artist, and ordered him to paint on the door of the smithy exactly such another demon as he had seen in the church. The artist painted it. Thenceforward the old man, every time he entered the smithy, always looked at the Demon and said, "Good morning, fellow-countryman!" And then he would lay the fire in the furnace and begin his work.

Well, the Smith lived in good accord with the Demon for some ten years. Then he fell ill and died. His son succeeded to his place as head of the household, and took the smithy into his own hands. But he was not disposed to show attention to the Demon as the old man had done. When he went into the smithy in the morning, he never said "Good morrow" to him; instead of offering him a kindly word, he took the biggest hammer he had handy, and thumped the Demon with it three times right on the forehead, and then he would go to his work. And when one of God's holy days came round, he would go to church and offer each saint a taper; but he would go up to the Demon and spit in his face. Thus three years went by, he all the while favoring the Evil One every morning either with a spitting or with a hammering. The Demon endured it and endured it, and at last found it past all endurance. It was too much for him.

"I've had quite enough of this insolence from him!" thinks he. "Suppose I make use of a little diplomacy, and play him some sort of a trick!"

So the Demon took the form of a youth, and went to the smithy.

"Good day, uncle!" says he.

"Good day!"

"What should you say, uncle, to taking me as an apprentice? At all events, I could carry fuel for you, and blow the bellows."

The Smith liked the idea. "Why shouldn't I?" he replied. "Two are better than one."

The Demon began to learn his trade; at the end of a month he knew more about smith's work than his master did himself, was able to do everything that his master couldn't do. It was a real pleasure to look at him! There's no describing how satisfied his master was with him, how fond he got of him. Sometimes the master didn't go into the smithy at all himself, but trusted entirely to his journeyman, who had complete charge of everything.

Well, it happened one day that the master was not at home, and the journeyman was left all by himself in the smithy. Presently he saw an old lady driving along the street in her carriage, whereupon he popped his head out of doors and began shouting:—

"Heigh, sirs! Be so good as to step in here! We've opened a new business here; we turn old folks into young ones."

Out of her carriage jumped the lady in a trice, and ran into the smithy.

"What's that you're bragging about? Do you mean to say it's true? Can you really do it?" she asked the youth.

"We haven't got to learn our business!" answered the Demon. "If I hadn't been able to do it, I wouldn't have invited people to try."

"And how much does it cost?" asked the lady.

"Five hundred roubles altogether."

"Well, then, there's your money; make a young woman of me."

The Demon took the money; then he sent the lady's coachman into the village.

"Go," says he, "and bring me here two buckets full of milk."

After that he took a pair of tongs, caught hold of the lady by the feet, flung her into the furnace, and burnt her up; nothing was left of her but her bare bones.

When the buckets of milk were brought, he emptied them into a large tub, then he collected all the bones and flung them into the milk. Just fancy! at the end of about three minutes the lady emerged from the milk—alive, and young, and beautiful!

Well, she got into her carriage and drove home. There she went straight to her husband, and he stared hard at her, but didn't know she was his wife.

"What are you staring at?" says the lady. "I'm young and elegant, you see, and I don't want to have an old husband! Be off at once to the smithy, and get them to make you young; if you don't, I won't so much as acknowledge you!"

There was no help for it; off set the seigneur. But by that time the Smith had returned home, and had gone into the smithy. He looked about; the journeyman wasn't to be seen. He searched and searched, he enquired and enquired, never a thing came of it; not even a trace of the youth could be found. He took to his work by himself, and was hammering away, when at that moment up drove the seigneur, and walked straight into the smithy.

"Make a young man of me," says he.

"Are you in your right mind, Barin? How can one make a young man of you?"

"Come, now! you know all about that."

"I know nothing of the kind."

"You lie, you scoundrel! Since you made my old woman young, make me young too; otherwise, there will be no living with her for me."

"Why I haven't so much as seen your good lady."

"Your journeyman saw her, and that's just the same thing. If he knew how to do the job, surely you, an old hand, must have learnt how to do it long ago. Come, now, set to work at once. If you don't, it will be the worse for you. I'll have you rubbed down with a birch-tree towel."

The Smith was compelled to try his hand at transforming the seigneur. He held a private conversation with the coachman as to how his journeyman had set to work with the lady, and what he had done to her, and then he thought:—

"So be it! I'll do the same. If I fall on my feet, good; if I don't, well, I must suffer all the same!"

So he set to work at once, stripped the seigneur naked, laid hold of him by the legs with the tongs, popped him into the furnace, and began blowing the bellows. After he had burnt him to a cinder, he collected his remains, flung them into the milk, and then waited to see how soon a youthful seigneur would jump out of it. He waited one hour, two hours. But nothing came of it. He made a search in the tub. There was nothing in it but bones, and those charred ones.

Just then the lady sent messengers to the smithy, to ask whether the seigneur would soon be ready. The poor Smith had to reply that the seigneur was no more.

When the lady heard that the Smith had only turned her husband into a cinder, instead of making him young, she was tremendously angry, and she called together her trusty servants, and ordered them to drag him to the gallows. No sooner said than done. Her servants ran to the Smith's house, laid hold of him, tied his hands together, and dragged him off to the gallows. All of a sudden there came up with them the youngster who used to live with the Smith as his journeyman, who asked him:—

"Where are they taking you, master?"

"They're going to hang me," replied the Smith, and straightway related all that had happened to him.

"Well, uncle!" said the Demon, "swear that you will never strike me with your hammer, but that you will pay me the same respect your father always paid, and the seigneur shall be alive, and young, too, in a trice."

The Smith began promising and swearing that he would never again lift his hammer against the Demon, but would always pay him every attention. Thereupon the journeyman hastened to the smithy, and shortly afterwards came back again, bringing the seigneur with him, and crying to the servants:

"Hold! hold! Don't hang him! Here's your master!"

Then they immediately untied the cords, and let the Smith go free.

From that time forward the Smith gave up spitting at the Demon and striking him with his hammer. The journeyman disappeared, and was never seen again.

But the seigneur and his lady entered upon a prosperous course of life, and if they haven't died, they're living still.

# STORY of VASILISA
## with the GOLDEN TRESS,
## and of IVAN THE PEA

**M**any years ago there lived a very celebrated czar. He had two sons and a beautiful daughter. This daughter lived in a high tower until she was twenty years of age. She was much beloved by the czar and czarina, and was a great favourite with her nurses and waiting-women. But not a single prince or knight had seen her, as she was never allowed to leave the tower, or to breathe the air of freedom. Her name was Vasilisa with the Golden Tress.

Vasilisa had many handsome dresses and rich jewels, but she was weary of them; the tower was confined, and sad and oppressed, she sighed for a change of scene. She had long, thick hair, of a golden hue, which was plaited into a single tress reaching to her feet: hence she was called Vasilisa with the Golden Tress.

News flies quickly over the wide world. Many czars, hearing of the princess's beauty, sent ambassadors to her father with offers of marriage. The czar was in no hurry; but when the proper time arrived, he sent messengers to all parts of the world to announce that the Princess Vasilisa would select a husband, and he therefore invited czars and princes to his court. Then he went to the tower, and told the beautiful Vasilisa what he had done.

The princess was greatly pleased, and looking through the golden bars of her chamber on to the beautiful garden full of flowers, she asked permission to go there with her maids to play.

"Father," she said, "I have never seen God's world, nor walked on the grass, nor among the flowers; nor have I ever seen your royal palace. Allow me to play in the garden with my nurses and maids."

The czar gave his permission at once. The beautiful Vasilisa descended from the high tower, and went into the courtyard; the door was opened, and the princess found herself in a green meadow which gradually rose to a steep hill; the hill was covered with trees, and the meadow with many coloured flowers. The princess plucked the lovely flowers as she went on, and ran a little in advance of her attendants. All at once there arose a strong wind, such as was neither known nor heard of before, such a wind as was never remembered by the oldest people,— it blew a perfect hurricane. In a moment the wind lifted the princess up and carried her away. The attendants screamed; some ran away in terror, others looked helplessly around them, and saw how the wind bore the beautiful Vasilisa with the Golden Tress out of their sight. It carried her over many countries and deep rivers, through three kingdoms into a fourth, which belonged to a terrible dragon.

The women ran into the palace, and falling on their knees before the czar, cried piteously,—

"Have mercy, and do not punish us! The wind has carried away our light—the beautiful Vasilisa with the Golden Tress—we know not whither!" And they told him all that had happened. The czar was very angry with them, and deeply grieved at the loss of his daughter; nevertheless, he forgave them all. On the following morning the foreign princes arrived, and seeing what grief was depicted on the czar's countenance, they enquired the cause of it.

"Woe is me!" cried the unhappy czar, "the wind has carried away my dear daughter Vasilisa with the Golden Tress, and I know not whither she has gone!" And he told them all that had happened.

When the princes heard this story they thought the czar had changed his mind, and no longer wished his daughter to marry; they therefore hastened into the tower formerly occupied by the princess, and searched everywhere, but could not find her.

The czar dismissed his visitors with all due honour, and gave a rich present to each of them; they mounted their horses and returned to their own countries.

The two young princes, brothers of Vasilisa, seeing the tears of their father and mother, said to them,—

"Father, and you, mother, give us your blessing, and permit us to go in search of your daughter and our sister."

"My dear sons," cried the afflicted czar, "where would you go?"

"We will go, father, in every direction; wherever the road will take us,—where the birds fly, and our eyes will guide us. Perhaps we shall find her."

The czar blessed them, and the czarina made everything ready for their journey; they all wept at parting, and then the princes set forth on their search. But whether they would have to travel near or far; whether for a long or a short time, the princes knew not.

They travelled for one year, they travelled for two years, and they passed through three kingdoms. Then, at a distance, they could see dark, high mountains, and among them a sandy wilderness, which was the country of the Dragon. The princes asked everywhere of those who passed by,—

"Have you heard or seen where the Princess Vasilisa with the Golden Tress is?" Everywhere the people answered, "We have neither seen nor heard where she is." Having thus replied, they went on their way.

The princes approached a large town; on the road thither they saw an old, lame man on crutches, carrying a wallet, who asked them for alms. The princes stopped, gave him some silver money, and enquired whether he had seen, or heard of, the Princess Vasilisa, the Unveiled Beauty with the Golden Tress.

"My young friends," answered the old man, "I see you are wanderers from a foreign land. Our czar, the Dragon, has forbidden us to talk with strangers. We may not tell to any one that the wind has brought a beautiful princess to this town."

When the princes heard that their sister was so near to them, they spurred their flagging steeds and galloped to the palace. It was truly a palace! It stood on a single silver pillar, and was made all of pure gold; the roof which covered it was of precious stones. The stairs leading to the entrance door spread out like two wings, but ran into one at the top; they were made of rare pearls. At that moment the beautiful Vasilisa was looking out of a window with golden bars, and recognising her brothers she screamed with delight. She then ordered them to be secretly admitted. Happily the Dragon was away, as the princess was greatly afraid lest he should see them; but no sooner had the princes come in than the silver pillar began to groan, the stairs to spread out, the roof to sparkle, and the whole castle to tremble and to turn round.

"The Dragon is coming!" cried the terrified princess. "At his approach the palace turns round and round. Hide, brothers, hide!"

No sooner had she uttered these words than the Dragon rushed hissing in, and demanded in a terrible voice, "Who is here?"

"We are here!" answered the princes fearlessly. "We have come for our sister Vasilisa."

"O-ho!" cried the Dragon, flapping his wings. "Since you have come to take your sister away, it will not be for nothing if I kill you. But, although you are the brothers of Vasilisa, you are no very terrible knights." And hissing and roaring he seized one of the brothers with his wings and hurled him against the other. The courtiers came in, took up the dead princes, and threw them into a deep ditch.

The princess burst into tears. Vasilisa would neither eat, nor drink, nor look upon the beautiful world around her. Three days thus passed away; but as she did not die, her resolution failed her, and she determined to live; she regretted to lose her beauty; she listened to the calls of hunger, and on the fourth day took some food.

The princess now began to think how she might possibly escape from the Dragon. One day she said to him coaxingly,—

"Dear Dragon, your strength is great, your wings far spreading and powerful; can no one withstand you?"

"My time is not yet come," said the Dragon. "It was written at the hour of my birth that the only being who could withstand me would be Ivan the Pea, grown up from a pea."

The Dragon laughed as he said this, not anticipating such an antagonist. The strong put confidence in their strength; but what is said in jest will sometimes become a truth.

Meanwhile, the czarina sorrowed for the loss of her daughter and of her two sons. One day she went with her ladies-in-waiting into the garden to try to amuse herself. It was hot, and the czarina became very thirsty. In the garden there was a beautiful well of spring water, flowing into a white marble basin. The czarina dipped a golden cup into the basin, and, drinking hastily, swallowed a pea with the water. In the course of time the czarina had a son, and he was called Ivan the Pea. He grew up not by years but by hours. He was a handsome boy,—strong and plump, full of spirit and play, ever laughing and springing on the sands, and daily increasing in strength.

At ten years of age, Ivan the Pea was a tall, powerful knight. He asked whether he had any sisters or brothers; and upon hearing that his sister Vasilisa had been carried away by the wind, and that his two brothers who went to seek her had never returned, he begged his parents to permit him to go also in search of them all.

"My dear son!" cried the czar and czarina, "you are still too young. Your brothers went away and never returned; if you leave us, you also will be lost."

"No," answered Ivan the Pea; "I shall not be lost. I desire of all things to find my brothers and sister."

His parents endeavoured to dissuade him from going, but all in vain. At last they gave their consent, blessed him with tears in their eyes, and bade him adieu.

Ivan the Pea set forth on his journey. He travelled for one day, he travelled for two; towards evening he entered a gloomy forest. In this forest there was a hut on hen's legs, shaken by the wind, and turning round and round. Following old custom and nursery tradition, Ivan blew upon it, saying,—

"Hut, hut, turn about, with your back to the forest and your front to me."

The hut immediately turned itself round with its front towards him. An old woman was looking out of the window, and she asked, "Whom have we here?"

Ivan bowed to her, and enquired whether she had observed which way the wind was in the habit of carrying beautiful girls.

"Ah, my son," said the old woman, coughing and looking hard at Ivan, "the wind has troubled me dreadfully. It is now a hundred and twenty years that I have lived in this hut, without ever once leaving it; it will kill me some day. You must know though that it is not the wind that is in fault, but the Dragon."

"Which is the way to him?"

"Take care; the Dragon will swallow you up."

"We shall see."

"Be mindful of your head, good knight," continued the old woman, shaking her toothless gums, "and promise me that, if you return safely, you will bring me some of the water from the Dragon's palace, in which, if I wash myself I shall be made young again."

"I promise; I will bring you some of the water, grandmother."

"I take your word for it. And now, my dear son, go towards the sunset; after a year's journeying you will arrive at the Fox's mountain; then ask the way to the Dragon's kingdom."

"Farewell, grandmother."

"Farewell, my son."

Ivan went towards the setting sun. A story is soon told, but a difficult work is not so soon completed. Having passed through three kingdoms he arrived at the Dragon's dominions. Before the gates of the city he saw an old, blind, and lame beggar with a wallet. Having given the beggar some alms, Ivan the Pea asked him whether in that city there did not live a young princess, called Vasilisa with the Golden Tress?

"Yes," said the beggar; "but we are forbidden to tell of it."

Upon hearing that his sister was indeed there, Ivan went at once to the palace. At that moment the beautiful Vasilisa with the Golden Tress was watching for the coming of the Dragon from the window. Seeing a young knight approaching, she sent to him secretly to learn his name, and to know whether he was not sent by her father or mother. When she heard that it was Ivan, her youngest brother, whom she had never seen before, the princess rushed out of the palace, and called to him with tears in her eyes,—

"Run, dearest brother! Fly from this place. The Dragon will soon be here, and will kill you!"

"Dearest sister, I am not afraid of the Dragon, nor of all his strength."

"Are you then the Pea, and therefore able to withstand him?"

"Wait a moment, sister; let me have something to drink first."

"And what will you drink, brother?"

"A bucketful of mead."

Vasilisa ordered a bucket of mead to be brought in, and Ivan drank it at a draught, without even once stopping to take breath; he then asked for more. The surprised princess ordered some more mead to be brought in.

"Now, brother," she said, "I believe that you are Ivan the Pea."

"Give me something to eat, dear sister, and then let me rest after my journey."

The princess then directed her servants to bring in a strong chair. Ivan sat down upon it, and it immediately broke into pieces. The attendants then brought another chair, still stronger, covered and joined together with iron. When Ivan sat down, it creaked and bent under him.

"Oh brother!" cried the princess, "that is the Dragon's own seat."

"It seems then," said Ivan smiling, "that I am heavier than he."

He then got up, went to an old sage, who was smith to the court, and ordered an iron staff to be made, to weigh five hundred *puds*.[1] The smiths set to work; hammered the iron night and day amid a shower of red-hot sparks, and in forty hours finished the staff. It required the united strength of fifty men to bring it to the castle. Ivan the Pea lifted it up with one hand, and threw it into the air. The air whistled as the staff passed through: it and disappeared in the clouds.

The inhabitants ran from place to place panic-stricken; they were afraid that the staff, falling down again, would crush their city into ruins, then roll into the sea, which would overflow and drown them all.

Prince Ivan gave orders that the people should let him know when the iron staff was seen falling again to the ground, and then went quietly into the palace. The terrified people fled away from the principal square. Some looked from their doors and windows to see whether the iron beam was about to descend. They waited one, they waited two hours; at the end of the third, word was sent to the palace that the staff was coming down. Ivan the Pea ran into the square, stretched out his

---

1. A *pud* is a weight of forty pounds.

hand and caught the staff as it fell. It came down with such force that it bent in his hand. The prince straightened it on his knee, and then returned to the castle.

Suddenly a dreadful hissing noise was heard; the Dragon was coming. His horse, the wind, flew with the swiftness of an arrow, vomiting forth flames. At a first glance the Dragon looked like a knight; but his head was that of a dragon. Usually at his approach, even if he were miles away, the palace would tremble, and move from place to place; now the Dragon observed, for the first time, that it did not stir. There must be a stranger within. The Dragon paused an instant— hissed and roared; his horse, the wind, shook his black mane and spread out his monstrous wings. The Dragon rushed to the palace, and the palace did not stir an inch.

"O-ho!" roared the Dragon, "I have to do with an enemy; perhaps it is the Pea."

Prince Ivan soon appeared.

"I will put you in the palm of one hand, clap my other hand upon you, and crush you to atoms!" cried the Dragon.

"We shall see," said Ivan, approaching with the staff.

"Begone from my castle!" roared the Dragon in a fury.

"Begone, you!" answered Ivan, lifting up his staff.

The Dragon flew up in the air that he might strike Prince Ivan and pierce him with his lance; but he missed his aim. The prince sprang aside, and exclaiming, "It is now my turn!" threw the staff at the Dragon with such force that the blow broke and scattered him into a thousand fragments. The staff pierced the earth, and passed through two kingdoms into a third.

The people threw up their caps with joy, and chose Ivan to be their czar. But Ivan, as a reward for the sage smith, who in so short a time had made him such a staff, ordered the old man to be called before him, and said to the people,—

"This is your czar; obey him for good as you once obeyed the Dragon for evil."

Then Ivan took some of the water of death and of the water of life, and sprinkled them over the bodies of his brothers. The young men rose up, and rubbing their eyes, exclaimed,—

"Heaven knows how long we have slept!"

"My dear brothers" said Ivan, embracing them tenderly, "without my help you would have slept for ages."

Then Ivan took some of the water of the Dragon, ordered a ship to be built, and sailing on the river Swan, with the beautiful Vasilisa with the Golden Tress, he passed through three kingdoms into a fourth,—his own country. He remembered the old woman in the hut, and gave her some of the water. When the old woman had washed herself in it she became young again; she sang and danced with joy, and accompanied Prince Ivan on his journey.

The czar and czarina received their son Ivan with great joy and honour. They sent messengers to all parts of the world, announcing that their daughter, the beautiful Vasilisa with the Golden Tress, had safely returned home. There were great rejoicings: bells rang merrily, trumpets sounded, drums were beaten, guns were fired. Vasilisa obtained a husband and Prince Ivan a wife. At the marriage feast there were mountains of meat and rivers of mead. They ordered four crowns to be made, and celebrated two weddings at once.

The great-grandfathers of our great-grandfathers were there; they drank of the mead and left some of it for us, but we have never tasted it. This, however, we heard: that after the death of the czar, Ivan the Pea ascended the throne; ruled the people with great glory; and the fame of Czar the Pea has been remembered from generation to generation.

# GO TO the VERGE of DESTRUCTION and BRING BACK SHMAT-RAZUM

I n a certain kingdom there lived a wifeless, unmarried king, who had a whole company of sharpshooters. They went to the forests, shot birds of passage, and furnished the king's table with game. Among these sharpshooters was one named Fedot, who hit the mark and almost never missed; for this reason the king loved him beyond all his comrades.

Once while shooting in the early morning, just at dawn, Fedot went into a dark, dense forest, and saw a blue dove sitting on a tree. He aimed, fired, struck her wing, and she fell to the damp earth. The sharpshooter picked her up, was going to twist her neck and put her in his bag, when the blue dove spoke: "Oh, brave youth, do not tear off my stormy little head, do not send me out of the white world! Better take me alive, carry me home, put me on the window, and watch. As soon as sleep comes upon me strike me that moment with the back of thy right hand, and thou wilt gain great fortune."

Fedot marvelled. "What can it mean?" thought he; "in seeming a bird, but she speaks with a human voice. Never has such a thing happened to me before."

He brought the bird home, placed her on the window, and stood waiting. After a short time the bird put her head under her wing and fell asleep. The sharpshooter struck her lightly with the back of his right hand. The blue dove fell to the floor, and became a soul-maiden so beautiful as not to be imagined nor described, but only told about in a tale. Such another beauty could not be found in the whole world.

Said she to the young man, the king's sharpshooter: "Thou hast known how to get me; now know how to live with me. Thou wilt be my wedded husband, and I thy God-given wife. I am not a blue dove, but a king's daughter."

They agreed. Fedot married her, and they lived together. He is happy with his young wife, but does not forget his service. Every morning at dawn he takes his gun, goes out into the forest, and shoots game, which he carries to the king's kitchen.

His wife sees that he is wearied from this hunting, and says: "Listen, my dear. I am sorry for thee. Every God-given day thou dost wander through forests and swamps, comest home wet and worn, and profit to us not a whit. What sort of a life is this? But I know something so that thou wilt not be without gain. Get of roubles two hundred, and we will correct the whole business."

Fedot rushed around to his friends, got a rouble from one, and two from another, till he had just two hundred. "Now," said his wife, "buy different kinds of silk for this money."

He bought the silk; she took it, and said: "Be not troubled; pray to God and lie down to sleep: the morning is wiser than the evening."

He lay down and fell asleep; his wife went out on the porch, opened her magic book, and two unknown youths appeared at once. "What dost thou wish? Command us."

"Take this silk, and in one single hour make a piece of such wonderful tapestry as has not been seen in the world; let the whole kingdom be embroidered on it, with towns, villages, rivers, and lakes."

They went to work, and not only in an hour, but in ten minutes they had the tapestry finished,—a wonder for all. They gave it to the sharpshooter's wife, and vanished in an instant just as if they never had been. In the morning she gave the tapestry to her husband. "Here," said she, "take this to the merchants' rows, sell it, but see that thou ask no price of thy own; take what they give."

Fedot went to the merchants' rows; a trader saw him, came up, and asked: "Well, my good man, is this article for sale?"

"It is."

"What's the price?"

"Thou art a dealer, name the price."

The merchant thought and thought, but could not fix a price. Now a second, a third, and a fourth came; no one could set a price on the tapestry. At this time the mayor of the palace was passing by and saw the crowd; wishing to know what the merchants were talking about, he jumped out of his carriage, came up to them, and said: "Good morning, merchants, dealers, guests from beyond the sea; what is the question?"

"Here is a piece of tapestry that we cannot value."

The mayor looked at the tapestry and marvelled himself. "Look here, sharpshooter," said he, "tell me in truth and sincerity where didst thou get such glorious tapestry?"

"My wife made it."

"How much must one give for it?"

"I know not myself; my wife told me to set no price on it, but what people would give, that would be ours."

"Well here are ten thousand for thee."

Fedot took the money and gave up the tapestry. The mayor was always near the person of the king, ate and drank at his table. When he went to the king's to dine he took the tapestry. "Would it not please your Majesty to see what a glorious piece of work I have bought to-day?"

The king looked; he saw his whole kingdom as if on the palm of his hand. He opened his mouth in amazement.

"This is indeed work; in all my life I have never seen such cunning art. Well, mayor, say what thou pleasest, but I shall not give this back to thee." Straightway the king took twenty-five thousand out of his pocket, placed the money in the mayor's hand, and hung the tapestry in the palace.

"That's nothing," thought the mayor; "I will order another still better." Straightway he galloped to find the sharpshooter, found his cottage, went in; and the moment he saw Fedot's wife he forgot himself, his errand, knew not why he had come. Before him was such a beauty that he would not take his eyes off her all his life; he would have looked and looked. He gazes on another man's wife, and in his head thought follows thought: "Where has it been seen, where heard of, that a simple soldier possessed such a treasure? Though I serve the king's person and rank as a general I have never beheld such beauty!"

The mayor came to his mind with difficulty, and went home, 'gainst his will. From that hour, from that time, he was not his own. Sleeping or waking, he thought only of the beautiful woman; he could neither eat nor drink, she was ever before his eyes. The king noticed the change, and asked: "What has come upon thee,—some grief?"

"Oh, your Majesty, I have seen the sharpshooter's wife; there is not such a beauty in the whole world! I am thinking of her all the time; I can neither eat nor drink, with no herb can I charm away my sorrow."

The desire came to the king to admire the woman himself. He ordered his carriage and drove to the soldier's quarters. He entered the room and saw unspeakable beauty. No matter who looked on the woman,—an old man, a youth; each was in love, lost his wits, a heart-flame pinched him. "Why," thought the king, "am I wifeless and single? Let me marry this beauty,—that is the thing. Why is she a sharpshooter's wife? It is her fate to be queen."

The king returned to his palace and said to the mayor: "Listen to me! Thou hast known how to show me this unimaginable beauty, now find the way to get rid of her husband; I want to marry her myself. And if thou dost not put him out of the way, blame thyself; for though thou art my faithful servant, thou'lt die on the gallows."

The mayor went his way sadder than before. How was he to "finish the sharpshooter?" he could not think. As he was going through back lanes and waste places, a Baba Yaga met him.

"Stop," said she, "servant of the king! I know all thy thoughts. If thou wilt, I will aid thee in this unavoidable sorrow."

"Aid me, grandmother, and I'll pay what thou wishest."

"The king has ordered thee to put an end to Fedot the sharpshooter. That would be easy enough, for he is simple, were it not for his wife, who is awfully cunning. Well, we'll give them such a riddle that it will not soon be explained. Go back to the king and say: 'Beyond the thrice-ninth land, in the thirtieth kingdom, is an island, on that island a deer with golden horns.' Let the king bring together half a hundred sailors,—the most good-for-nothing fellows, all bitter drunkards,—and order that a rotten old ship which has been out of service for thirty years be fitted for the voyage. Let him send Fedot the sharpshooter on that ship to get the deer with golden horns. In order to go to the island it is necessary to sail neither more nor less than three years, and back from the island three more; six in all. Well, the ship will sail out on the sea, serve about a month, and sink right there; the sharpshooter and the sailors will go to the bottom, every man!"

The mayor listened to these words, thanked the Baba Yaga for her counsel, rewarded her with gold, and went off on a run to the king. "Your Majesty," said he, "Fedot can be finished in such and such fashion."

The king consented, and issued an order at once to the navy to prepare for a voyage an old rotten ship, to provision it for six years, and man it with fifty sailors, the most dissolute and bitter drunkards. Messengers ran to all the dram-shops and drinking-houses, collected such sailors that it was dear and precious to look at them. One had a black eye, another had his nose driven to one side.

As soon as it was reported to the king that the ship was ready, he sent for the sharpshooter and said: "Now, Fedot, thou art a hero of mine,—the first shot in the company. Do me a service. Go beyond the thrice-ninth land to the thirtieth kingdom. In that place is an island, on that island lives the deer with golden horns. Take it alive, and bring it to me."

Fedot became thoughtful, knew not what to answer.

"Think, think not," said the king; "but if thou do not the work, I have a sword, and thy head leaves thy shoulders!"

Fedot wheeled round to the left and went forth from the palace, came home in the evening powerfully sad, not wishing to utter one word.

"Why dost thou grieve, my dearest?" asked his wife. "Is there some mishap?"
He told her all.

"This is why thou art grieved. There is reason, indeed; for it is an exploit, not a service. Pray to God and lie down to sleep; the morning is wiser than the evening: everything will be done."

The sharpshooter lay down and slept. But his wife opened her magic-book, at once two unknown youths appeared before her and asked: "What dost thou wish? What dost thou need?"

"Go beyond the thrice-ninth land to the thirtieth kingdom, to an island; seize there the deer with golden horns, and bring it here."

"We obey; it will be done before dawn."

They rushed like a whirlwind to the island, caught the deer with golden horns, and brought it straight to Fedot's house. An hour before daybreak all was done, and they vanished as if they had never been. The beautiful wife roused her husband at dawn and said: "Look out; the deer with golden horns is walking in the yard. Take it with thee on board the ship, sail forward five days, on the sixth turn back."

The sharpshooter put the deer in a close, fastened cage, and had it carried on board the ship.

"What's there?" asked the sailors.

"Oh, supplies and medicine! It's a long voyage; we shall need many a thing."

The day for sailing came. A great crowd of people went to see the ship leave the wharf. The king went himself, made Fedot chief over all the sailors, and bade him farewell.

The vessel sailed five days on the sea; the shores had long vanished. Fedot ordered a hundred-and-twenty-gallon cask to be rolled on to the deck, and said to the sailors: "Drink, brothers; spare it not, your souls are your measure!"

They were delighted, rushed to the cask, began to drink, and got so drunk that they rolled down on the deck, and fell fast asleep at the side of the cask. Fedot took the helm, turned the ship around toward the harbor, and sailed home. So that the sailors should not know anything about it, he kept pouring liquor into them from morning till night; when they began to open their eyes after one drunken fit, a new cask was ready. On the eleventh day the ship drew up at the wharf; the flag was hoisted, and guns fired. The king heard the firing, and ran down to the landing. "What does all this mean?" He saw the sharpshooter, fell into a towering passion, and rushed at him furiously. "How hast thou dared to come back before time?"

"But where was I to go, your Majesty? Some fool might have spent ten years in sailing over the seas and got nothing; but I, instead of spending six years, did the work in ten days. Would you be pleased to look at the golden-horned deer?"

Straightway they brought the cage from the ship and let out the golden-horned deer. The king saw that the sharpshooter was right; he could not touch him, he let him go home. The sailors had a holiday for six years; no one could ask them to work during that time, for the voyage was counted as six years, and they had served their time.

Next day the king called the mayor into his presence and threatened him: "What meanest thou; art making sport of me? 'Tis clear thy head is not dear to thee. Do what thou pleasest, but find means of putting Fedot to a cruel death."

"Let me think, your Majesty; we may mend matters." The mayor went his way, betook himself to back lanes and waste places, met the Baba Yaga.

"Stop, servant of the king! I know thy thoughts: dost wish I will help thee in trouble?"

"Oh, help me, grandmother! Fedot has brought the deer with golden horns."

"Oh, I have heard that already. It would be as easy to put Fedot out of the way as to take a pinch of snuff, for he is simple; but his wife is terribly cunning. Well, we'll give them another riddle that they will not solve so quickly. Tell the king to send the sharpshooter to the verge of destruction and bring back Shmat-Razum,—that's a task he will not accomplish to all eternity; he will either be lost without tidings, or come back empty-handed."

The mayor rewarded the old witch with gold and hurried to the king, who heard him and summoned Fedot.

"Fedot," said the king, "thou art a hero, the best shot I have. Thou hast brought me the deer with golden horns, now thou must do me another service; and if thou wilt not do it, I have a sword, and thy head leaves thy shoulders. Thou must go to the verge of destruction and bring back Shmat-Razum."

Fedot turned to the left, walked out of the palace, went home sad and thoughtful.

"My dear," asked his wife, "why art thou sad, has some misfortune happened?"

"Ah," said he, "one woe has rolled from my neck and another rolled on! The king sends me to the verge of destruction to bring back Shmat-Razum. For thy beauty I bear all this trouble and care."

"That," said she, "is no small task,—nine years to go there, and nine to come back, eighteen in all. Will good come of it? God knows. But pray to the Lord and lie down to sleep; the morning is wiser than the evening. To-morrow thou'lt know all."

After Fedot had lain down, his wife opened her magic book and asked the two unknown youths if they knew how to go to the verge of destruction and bring back Shmat-Razum. They answered: "We know not." In the morning she roused her husband and said, "Go to the king and ask for the road golden treasure,—thou hast eighteen years to wander; when thou hast the money come home for the parting."

Fedot got the money from the king and returned to take farewell of his wife. She gave him a towel and a ball, and said: "When thou goest out of the town throw the ball down before thee, and wherever it rolls do thou follow. Here is a towel of my own work; no matter where thou art, wipe thy face with it after washing."

Fedot took farewell of his wife and comrades, bowed down on all four sides, and went beyond the barrier. He threw down the ball before him; it rolled, rolled on, and he followed after.

About a month had passed, when the king summoned the mayor and said: "The sharpshooter has gone to wander over the white world for eighteen years; it is evident that he will not come back alive. Eighteen years, as thou knowest, are not two weeks; many a thing may happen on the road. He has much money, and robbers will fall upon him perhaps, strip him, and give him to a savage death. I think we can begin at his wife now. Take my carriage, drive to the soldier's quarters, and bring her to the palace."

The mayor drove to Fedot's house, entered, saluted the sharpshooter's wife, and said: "Hail, witty woman, the king has ordered us to present thee at the palace."

She went. The king received her with gladness, led her to a golden chamber, and spoke these words: "Dost thou wish to be queen? I will take thee in marriage."

"Where has it ever been seen or heard of," asked she, "that a wife was taken from her living husband? Though he is a simple soldier he is my lawful husband."

"If thou wilt not yield of thy free will, I will take thee by force."

The beautiful woman laughed, struck the floor, became a blue dove, and flew out through the window.

Fedot journeyed over many lands and kingdoms, the ball rolling ahead of him all the time. When he came to a river the ball became a bridge; whenever he wanted rest it became a soft couch. Whether it is long or short, a story is soon told, but a deed is not soon done; the sharpshooter arrived at a splendid palace, the ball rolled to the gate and disappeared. Fedot went straight up the stairs into a rich chamber, where he was met by three maidens of unspeakable loveliness.

"Whence comest, good man, and for what?"

"Oh, beautiful maidens, ye have not let me rest after the long journey, but have begun to inquire. First ye should give me to eat and drink, put me to rest, and then make inquiry."

Straightway they set the table. When he had eaten and drunk and rested, they brought him water, a basin, and an embroidered towel. He took not the towel, but said, "I have one of my own." When they saw it they asked: "Good man, where didst thou get that towel?"

"My wife gave it me."

"Then thy wife is our own sister."

They called their aged mother. The moment she saw the towel she recognized it. "Why, this is my daughter's work." She asked the guest all sorts of questions. He told her how he had married her daughter, and how the king had sent him to the verge of destruction to bring back Shmat-Razum.

"Oh, my dear son-in-law, of that wonder even I have not heard! Wait a moment; maybe my servants have."

She went out on the balcony and called in a loud voice. Presently all kinds of beasts ran up, and all kinds of birds flew to her. "Hail to you, beasts of the wilderness, birds of the air! Ye beasts run through all places, ye birds fly everywhere; have ye never heard how to go to the verge of destruction, where Shmat-Razum lives?"

All the beasts and birds answered in one voice: "No; we have never heard!"

Then the old woman sent them all to their homes in hidden places, forests, and thickets; went to her magic book, opened it, and that instant two giants appeared. "What is thy pleasure; what dost thou wish?"

"This, my faithful servants,—bear my son-in-law and me to the ocean sea wide, and stop just in the middle above the very abyss."

Immediately they seized the sharpshooter and the old woman and bore them on like a stormy whirlwind till they stopped just in the middle above the abyss. They stood up themselves like pillars, holding the old woman and the sharpshooter in their arms. The old woman cried out with a loud voice, and all the fishes and living things in the sea swam to her in such multitudes that the blue sea could not be seen for them: "Hail, fish and worms of the sea! Ye swim in all places, ye pass by all islands; have ye not heard how to go to the verge of destruction, where lives Shmat-Razum?"

All worms and fishes answered in one voice, "No; we've not heard!"

All at once an old limping frog, who had been thirty years out of service, pushed her way to the front and said, "Kwa-kwa! I know where to find such a wonder!"

"Well, then, my dear, thou art the person I need," said the old woman. She took the frog, and commanded the giants to bear them home. They were at the palace in a flash. The old woman asked the frog how her son was to go.

"Oh!" said the frog, "that place is at the rim of the world,—far, far away. I would conduct him myself, but I am very old; I can barely move my legs,—I couldn't jump there in fifty years."

The old woman took a bowl with some fresh milk, put the frog in it, gave the bowl to Fedot, and said: "Carry this in thy hand; she will show thee the way."

The sharpshooter took farewell of the old woman and her daughters, and went on his journey, the frog showing him the way. Whether it was near or distant, long or short, he came at last to a flaming river, beyond which was a lofty mountain with a door in the side.

"Kwa-kwa!" said the frog. "Put me down out of the bowl; we must cross the river."

He put her on the ground.

"Now, good youth, sit thou on my back; do not spare me."

He sat on her back and pressed her to the ground; she began to swell, and swelled until she was as big as a stack of hay. The sharpshooter's one care was to keep from falling. "If I fall," thought he, "I shall be crushed." The frog cleared the flaming river at a jump, became small as before, and said: "Now, good youth, I will wait here; but do thou enter that door in the mountain. Thou wilt find a cave,— hide thyself well. After a time two old men will come in: listen to what they say, and watch what they do; when they are gone, act as they did."

The sharpshooter entered the door of the mountain; it was so dark in the cave that if a man strained his eyes out he could not see a thing. Fedot felt around and found a cupboard, crept in. After a while two old men entered and said, "Shmat-Razum, feed us!"

That moment, however it happened, the lamps were lighted, the dishes and plates rattled, and various kinds of food and wine appeared on the table. The old men ate and drank, and then ordered Shmat-Razum to remove everything. Everything disappeared in a flash; neither table, nor food, nor wine, nor lights remained. The two old men went out.

The sharpshooter crawled from the cupboard and cried, "Hei, Shmat-Razum!"

"What dost thou wish?"

"Feed me!"

Again the lights, the table, the food and drink appeared as before. Fedot sat at the table and said: "Hei, Shmat-Razum, sit down brother, with me, we'll eat and drink together; it is irksome for me alone."

The voice of the unseen answered: "Oh, kind man! whence has God brought thee? It is nearly thirty years that I serve these old men in faith and in truth, and all this time they have never once seated me with themselves."

The sharpshooter looked and wondered. He saw no one, but the food was swept from the plates as if with a broom; the bottles raised themselves and poured the wine into glasses,—behold, in a moment bottles and glasses are empty!

"Shmat-Razum, dost thou wish to serve me?" asked the sharpshooter. "I'll give thee a pleasant life."

"Why not? I am sick of being here; and thou, I see, art a kind man."

"All right; pick up everything and come along." The sharpshooter went out of the cave, looked around, saw no one, and asked: "Art thou here, Shmat-Razum?"

"Here; I'll not leave thee, never fear."

"Very well," said Fedot, and sat on the frog,—she swelled, jumped over the river, and became small. He put her in the bowl, and went on the homeward road, came to his mother-in-law, and made his new servant entertain the old woman and her daughters. Shmat-Razum gave them such a feast that the old woman came very near dancing from joy. She ordered that three bowls of milk be given to the frog every day in reward for her faithfulness. The sharpshooter bade good by to his friends and set out for home. He travelled and journeyed till he was almost wearied to death. "Oh, Shmat-Razum," said he, "if thou couldst only know how tired I am, I am just losing my legs."

"Why not tell me long ago?" asked the other; "I should have brought thee home quickly." With that he seized Fedot and bore him like a rushing whirlwind, so swiftly that his cap fell off.

"Hei, Shmat-Razum, wait a minute; my cap is gone."

"Late, my master; thy cap is now three thousand miles behind."

Towns and villages, rivers and forests, just flashed before the eye; as Fedot was flying over a deep sea Shmat-Razum said: "If thou wishest, I will make a summer-house in the midst of the sea; thou canst rest, and acquire great fortune."

"Well, make it."

They dropped down toward the sea, and behold, where a moment before the waves were rolling, an island rose up, and in the centre a golden pleasure-house.

"Now, my master, sit down in this house, rest, and look at the sea. Presently three merchant-ships will sail by and cast anchor. Invite the merchants, entertain them well, and exchange me for three wonderful things which they have. I'll come to thee again in my own time."

Fedot looked; three merchant-ships were sailing from the west. The merchants saw the island and wondered.

"What does this mean?" asked they. "How many times have we sailed by here and seen nothing but water, and now an island and a pleasure-house! Let us stand up to the shore, brothers, let us look and admire."

They stopped the ships, cast anchor; the three merchants stepped into a light boat, went to the island, landed, and saluted Fedot,—

"Hail, worthy man!"

"Good health to you, foreign merchants! We crave kindness. Come in, rejoice, have a good time, and rest yourselves. This pleasure-house was made on purpose for passing guests." They went in and sat down.

"Hei, Shmat-Razum, meat and drink!" A table appeared; on the table wines and meats, whatever the soul could desire was at hand in a moment. The merchants opened their mouths in amazement.

"Let us exchange," said they. "Give us thy servant, and take any one of our wonders."

"What wonders have ye?"

"Look, and thou wilt see."

One merchant took a small box from his pocket and opened it: that minute a glorious garden was spread over the whole island with flowers and paths; he closed the box, and the garden was gone. The second merchant took an axe from under his skirts and began to hit, hit strike, a ship came out: hit strike—another ship. He struck a hundred times—a hundred ships. They moved around the island under full canvas, with sailors and cannon. The sailors run and fire guns. The commanders come to the merchant for orders. He amused himself, hid his axe: the ships vanished from the eye, were as if they had never been. The third merchant took a horn, blew into it at one end: that minute an army appeared, cavalry and infantry, with muskets and cannons and flags; from every regiment come reports to the merchant, and he gives them orders. The army marches, with music sounding and banners waving. The merchant took his horn, blew in at the other end: there is nothing. Where has all the power gone to?

"Your wonders are strange," said the sharpshooter; "but these are all playthings for kings, and I am a simple soldier. If ye will exchange, however, I agree to give you my unseen servant for all three of your wonders."

"Is not that rather too much?"

"Well, ye know your own business, I suppose; but I will not exchange on other conditions."

The merchants thought to themselves, "What good are these ships and soldiers and garden to us? Let us exchange,—at least we shall have enough to eat and drink all our lives without trouble."

They gave the sharpshooter their wonders, and asked: "Shmat-Razum, wilt thou come with us?"

"Why not? It's all the same to me where I live."

The merchants returned to their ships and said: "Now, Shmat-Razum, fly about; give us to eat and drink." They invited all the men, and had such a feast that every one got drunk and slept a sound sleep.

The sharpshooter was sitting in the golden summer-house; he fell to thinking, and said: "I am sorry; where art thou now, trusty servant?"

"Here, my master."

Fedot rejoiced. "Isn't it time for us to go home?" The moment he spoke he was borne through the air as if by a whirlwind.

The merchants woke up, and wishing to drink off the effects of their carousal, cried out: "Give us to drink, Shmat-Razum." No one answered, nothing was brought; no matter how much they screamed and commanded, no result. "Well, gentlemen, this scoundrel has swindled us. Now Satan himself could not find him; the island has vanished, the pleasure-house is gone." The merchants grieved and regretted; then hoisted their sails and went to where they had business.

The sharpshooter soon arrived at his own kingdom, came down by the seashore. "Shmat-Razum, canst thou build me a palace here?"

"Why not?—it will be ready directly."

The palace appeared so splendid that it could not be described,—twice as good as the king's. Now the box was opened, and all around the palace was a glorious garden, with rare trees and flowers.

The sharpshooter sat by the window admiring the garden when all at once a blue dove flew in through the open window, struck the floor, and became his young wife. They embraced and kissed each other; then made inquiries and gave answer. Said his wife to Fedot: "Since the time thou didst leave me I have lived a lone dove in the forests and thickets."

Next morning the king went out on the balcony, and saw by the shore of the blue sea a new palace, and a green garden around it. "What insolent fellow has built on my land without leave?" Couriers hastened, discovered, reported, that the palace was built by Fedot, who was living there then, and with him his wife.

The king's anger increased. He gave orders to collect troops and go to the sea-shore, destroy the garden, break the palace into small pieces, and give the sharpshooter and his wife to a cruel death.

Fedot saw the strong army approaching. He took his axe quickly, and struck; a ship came forth; he struck a hundred times,—a hundred ships were ready; he blew his horn once, infantry was marching; he blew it a second time, cavalry was galloping. The commanders rushed to him from the ships, from the army, for orders. He ordered them to give battle. The music sounded at once, the drums rattled, the regiments advanced. The hundred ships open a cannonade on the king's capital. The army moves on at the sound of music and beat of drum. The infantry rout the king's soldiers, the cavalry take them prisoners. The king sees that his army is fleeing, hurries forward himself to stop it. But what could he do? Half an hour had not passed before he was killed.

When the battle was over, the people came together and begged the sharpshooter to take the government of the kingdom into his hands. He agreed, became king, and his wife queen.

*A*
HELPING
HAND

# THE BOOK of MAGIC

A soldier was quartered in a certain town. He had taken to study the Black Art, and had got possession of books which dealt therewith. One day, during his absence from his quarters, one of his comrades came to see him. Not finding him at home, the visitor took up one of the soldier's books, and for want of other occupation began to read it. It was in the evening, and he read by the light of a lamp. The book was full of names and nothing else. He had read about half of the names when he raised his head, and looking around him, saw that the room was full of diabolical looking beings. The soldier was struck with terror, and not knowing what to do, began again to read the book. After reading for some little time, he again looked round him; the number of spirts had increased. Again he read, and having finished the book, looked again around him. By this time the number of demons had so much increased that there was barely space for them in the room. They sat upon each other's shoulders, and pressed continually forward round the reader. The soldier saw that the situation was serious; he shut the book, closed his eyes, and anxiously awaited his comrade. The spirits pressed closer and closer upon him, crying,—

"Give us work to do—quick!"

The soldier reflected awhile, and then said,—

"Fill up the cisterns of all the baths in the town with water brought thither in a sieve."

The demons flew away. In two minutes they returned and said,—

"It is done! Give us some more work to do—quick!"

"Pull the Voivode's[1] house down, brick by brick—but take care you do not touch or disturb the inmates; then build it up again as it was before."

The goblins disappeared, but in two minutes returned.

"It is done!" they cried. "Give us more work—quick!"

"Go," said the soldier, "and count the grains of sand that lie at the bottom of the Volga, the number of drops of water that are in the river, and of the fish that swim in it, from its source to its mouth."

The spirits flew away; but in another minute they returned, having executed their task. Thus, before the soldier could think of some new labour to be done, the old one was completed, and the demons were again at his side demanding more work. When he began to think what he should give them, they pressed round him, and threatened him with instant death if he did not give them something to do. The soldier was becoming exhausted, and there was yet no sign of his comrade's return. What course should he take? How deliver himself from the evil spirits? The soldier thought to himself,—

"While I was reading the book, not one of the demons came near me. Let me try to read it again; perhaps that will keep them off."

Again he began to read the book of magic, but he soon observed that as he read the number of phantoms increased, so that soon such a host of the spirit-world surrounded him that the very lamp was scarcely visible. When the soldier hesitated at a word, or paused to rest himself, the goblins became more restless and violent, demanding,—

"Give us work to do! Give us work!"

The soldier was almost worn out, and unhappily knew not how to help himself. Suddenly a thought occurred to him,—

"The spirits appeared when I read the book from the beginning; let me now read it from the end, perhaps this well send them way."

He turned the book round and began to read it from the end. After reading for some time he observed that the number of spirits decreased; the lamp began again to burn brightly, and there was an empty space around him.

---

1. Governor

The soldier was delighted, and continued his reading. He read and read until he had read them all away. And thus he saved himself from the demons. His comrade came in soon afterwards. The soldier told him what had happened.

"It is fortunate for you," said his comrade, "that you began to read the book backwards in time. Had you not thus read them away by midnight they would have devoured you."

# IVAN TSAREVICH,
## the FIRE-BIRD,
## and the GRAY WOLF

In a certain kingdom, in a certain land, lived Tsar Vwislav Andronovich; he had three sons,—Dmitri Tsarevich, Vassili Tsarevich, and Ivan Tsarevich. Tsar Vwislav had a garden so rich that in no land was there better. In the garden grew many precious trees, with fruit and without fruit.

Tsar Vwislav had one favorite apple-tree, and on that tree grew apples all golden. The Fire-bird used to fly to the garden of Tsar Vwislav. She had wings of gold, and eyes like crystals of the East; and she used to fly to that garden every night, sit on the favorite apple-tree, pluck from it golden apples, and then fly away.

The Tsar grieved greatly over that apple-tree because the Fire-bird plucked from it many apples. Therefore he called his three sons and said: "My dear children, whichever one of you can catch the Fire-bird in my garden and take her alive, to him will I give during my life one half of the kingdom, and at my death I will give it all."

Then the sons cried out in one voice: "Gracious sovereign, our father, we will try with great pleasure to take the Fire-bird alive."

The first night Dmitri Tsarevich went to watch in the garden, and sat under the apple-tree from which the Fire-bird had been plucking the apples. He fell asleep, and did not hear the Fire-bird when she came, nor when she plucked many apples.

Next morning Tsar Vwislav called his son Dmitri Tsarevich, and asked, "Well, my dear son, hast thou seen the Fire-bird?"

"No, gracious sovereign, my father, she came not last night."

The next night Vassili Tsarevich went to the garden to watch the Fire-bird. He sat under the same apple-tree, and in a couple of hours fell asleep so soundly that he did not hear the Fire-bird when she came nor when she plucked apples.

Next morning Tsar Vwislav called him and asked, "Well, my dear son, hast thou seen the Fire-bird?"

"Gracious sovereign, my father, she came not last night."

The third night Ivan Tsarevich went to watch in the garden, and sat under the same apple-tree. He sat an hour, a second, and a third. All at once the whole garden was lighted up as if by many fires. The Fire-bird flew hither, perched on the apple-tree, and began to pluck apples. Ivan stole up to her so warily that he caught her tail, but could not hold the bird, she tore off, flew away; and there remained in the hand of Ivan Tsarevich but one feather of the tail, which he held very firmly.

Next morning, the moment Tsar Vwislav woke from his sleep, Ivan Tsarevich went to him and gave him the feather of the Fire-bird. The Tsar was greatly delighted that his youngest son had been able to get even one feather of the Fire-bird. This feather was so wonderful and bright that when carried into a dark chamber it shone as if a great multitude of tapers were lighted in that place. Tsar Vwislav put the feather in his cabinet as a thing to be guarded forever. From that time forth the Fire-bird flew to the garden no more.

Tsar Vwislav again called his sons, and said: "My dear children, I give you my blessing. Set out, find the Fire-bird, and bring her to me alive; and what I promised at first he will surely receive who brings me the bird."

Dmitri and Vassili Tsarevich began to cherish hatred against their youngest brother because he had pulled the feather from the tail of the Fire-bird. They took their father's blessing, and both went to find the Fire-bird. Ivan Tsarevich too began to beg his father's blessing. The Tsar said to him: "My dear son, my darling child, thou art still young, unused to such a long and difficult journey: why shouldst thou part from me? Thy brothers have gone; now, if thou goest too, and all three of you fail to return for a long time (I am old, and walk under God), and if during your absence the Lord takes my life, who would rule in my place? There might be rebellion too, or disagreement among our people,—there would be no one to stop it; or if an enemy should invade our land, there would be no one to command our men."

But no matter how the Tsar tried to detain Ivan Tsarevich, he could not avoid letting him go at his urgent prayer. Ivan Tsarevich took a blessing of his father, chose a horse, and rode away; he rode on, not knowing himself whither.

Riding by the path by the road, whether it was near or far, high or low, a tale is soon told, but a deed's not soon done. At last he came to the green meadows. In the open field a pillar stands, and on the pillar these words are written: "Whoever goes from the pillar straight forward will be hungry and cold; whoever goes to the right hand will be healthy and well, but his horse will be dead; whoever goes to the left hand will be killed himself, but his horse will be living and well." Ivan read the inscription, and went to the right hand, holding in mind that though his horse might be killed, he would remain alive, and might in time get another horse.

He rode one day, a second, and a third. All at once an enormous gray wolf came out against him and said: "Oh! is that thou, tender youth, Ivan Tsarevich? Thou hast read on the pillar that thy horse will be dead: why hast thou come hither, then?" The wolf said these words, tore Ivan Tsarevich's horse in two, and went to one side.

Ivan grieved greatly for his horse. He cried bitterly, and went forward on foot. He walked all day, and was unspeakably tired. He was going to sit down and rest, when all at once the Gray Wolf caught up with him and said: "I am sorry for thee, Ivan Tsarevich, thou art tired from walking; I am sorry that I ate thy good steed. Well, sit on me, the old wolf, and tell me whither to bear thee, and why."

Ivan Tsarevich told the Gray Wolf whither he had to go, and the Gray Wolf shot ahead with him swifter than a horse. After a time, just at nightfall, he brought Ivan Tsarevich to a stone wall not very high, halted, and said: "Now, Ivan Tsarevich, come down from the Gray Wolf, climb over that stone wall; on the other side is a garden, and in the garden the Fire-bird, in a golden cage. Take the Fire-bird, but touch not the cage. If thou takest the cage, thou'lt not escape; they will seize thee straightway."

Ivan Tsarevich climbed over the wall into the garden, saw the Fire-bird in the golden cage, and was greatly tempted by the cage. He took the bird out, and was going back; but changed his mind, and thought, "Why have I taken the bird without the cage? Where can I put her?" He returned; but had barely taken down the cage when there was a hammering and thundering throughout the whole garden, for there were wires attached to the cage. The watchmen woke up at that moment, ran to the garden, caught Ivan Tsarevich with the Fire-bird, and took him to the Tsar, who was called Dolmat. Tsar Dolmat was terribly enraged at Ivan, and shouted at him in loud, angry tones: "Is it not a shame for thee, young man, to steal? But who art thou, of what land, of what father a son, and how do they call thee by name?"

Ivan Tsarevich replied: "I am from Vwislav's kingdom, the son of Tsar Vwislav Andronovich, and they call me Ivan Tsarevich. Thy Fire-bird used to fly to our garden each night and pluck golden apples from my father's favorite apple-tree, and destroyed almost the whole tree. Therefore my father has sent me to find the Fire-bird and bring it to him."

"Oh, youthful young man, Ivan Tsarevich," said Tsar Dolmat, "is it fitting to do as thou hast done? Thou shouldst have come to me, and I would have given thee the Fire-bird with honor; but now will it be well for thee when I send to all lands to declare how dishonorably thou hast acted in my kingdom? Listen, however, Ivan Tsarevich. If thou wilt do me a service,—if thou wilt go beyond the thrice ninth land to the thirtieth kingdom and get for me from Tsar Afron the golden-maned steed, I will forgive thy offence and give thee the Fire-bird with great honor; if not, I will publish in all kingdoms that thou art a dishonorable thief."

Ivan Tsarevich went away from Tsar Dolmat in great grief, promising to obtain for him the golden-maned steed.

He came to the Gray Wolf, and told him all that Tsar Dolmat had said.

"Oh! is that thou, youthful young man, Ivan Tsarevich? Why didst thou disobey my words and take the golden cage?"

"I have offended in thy sight," said Ivan to the Gray Wolf.

"Well, let that go; sit on me, and I will take thee wherever thou wilt."

Ivan Tsarevich sat on the back of the Gray Wolf. The wolf was as swift as an arrow, and ran, whether it was long or short, till he came at last to the kingdom of Tsar Afron in the night-time. Coming to the white-walled stables, the Gray

Wolf said: "Go, Ivan Tsarevich, into these white-walled stables (the grooms on guard are sleeping soundly), and take the golden-maned steed. On the wall hangs a golden bridle; but take not the bridle, or it will go ill with thee."

Ivan Tsarevich entered the white-walled stables, took the steed, and was coming back; but he saw on the walls the golden bridle, and was so tempted that he took it from the nail. That moment there went a thunder and a noise throughout the stables, because strings were tied to the bridle. The grooms on guard woke up that moment, rushed in, seized Ivan Tsarevich, and took him to Tsar Afron. Tsar Afron began to question him. "Oh, youthful young man, tell me from what land thou art, of what father a son, and how do they call thee by name?"

To this Ivan Tsarevich replied: "I am from Vwislav's kingdom, the son of Tsar Vwislav, and they call me Ivan Tsarevich."

"Oh, youthful young man, Ivan Tsarevich!" said Tsar Afron, "was that which thou hast done the deed of an honorable knight? I would have given thee the golden-maned steed with honor. But now will it be well for thee when I send to all lands a declaration of how dishonorably thou hast acted in my kingdom? Hear me, however, Ivan Tsarevich: if thou wilt do me a service and go beyond the thrice ninth land to the thirtieth kingdom and bring to me Princess Yelena the Beautiful, with whom I am in love heart and soul for a long time, but whom I cannot obtain, I will pardon thy offence and give thee the golden-maned steed with honor. And if thou wilt not do me this service, I will declare in all lands that thou art a dishonorable thief."

Ivan Tsarevich promised Tsar Afron to bring Yelena the Beautiful, left the palace, and fell to crying bitterly.

He came to the Gray Wolf and told him all that had happened.

"Oh, Ivan Tsarevich, thou youthful young man," said the Gray Wolf, "why didst thou disobey me and take the golden bridle?"

"I have offended in thy sight," said Ivan Tsarevich.

"Well, let that go," replied the Wolf. "Sit on me; I will take thee wherever need be."

Ivan Tsarevich sat on the back of the Gray Wolf, who ran as swiftly as an arrow flies, and he ran in such fashion as to be told in a tale no long time; and at last he came to the kingdom of Yelena the Beautiful. Coming to the golden fence which surrounded her wonderful garden, the Wolf said: "Now, Ivan Tsarevich, come down from me and go back by the same road along which we came and wait in the field, under the green oak."

Ivan Tsarevich went where he was commanded. But the Gray Wolf sat near the golden fence, and waited till Yelena the Beautiful should walk in the garden.

Toward evening, when the sun was sinking low in the west, therefore, it was not very warm in the air, Princess Yelena went to walk in the garden with her maidens and court ladies. When she entered the garden and approached the place where the Gray Wolf was sitting behind the fence, he jumped out suddenly, caught the princess, sprang back again, and bore her away with all his power and might. He came to the green oak in the open field where Ivan Tsarevich was waiting, and said, "Ivan Tsarevich, sit on me quickly." Ivan sat on him, and the Gray Wolf bore them both along swiftly to the kingdom of Tsar Afron.

The nurses and maidens and all the court ladies who had been walking in the garden with the princess Yelena the Beautiful ran straightway to the palace and sent pursuers to overtake the Gray Wolf; but no matter how they ran, they could not overtake him, and turned back.

Ivan Tsarevich while sitting on the Gray Wolf with princess Yelena the Beautiful came to love her with his heart, and she Ivan Tsarevich; and when the Gray Wolf arrived at the kingdom of Tsar Afron, and Ivan Tsarevich had to take Yelena the Beautiful to the palace and give her to Tsar Afron, he grew very sad, and began to weep tearfully.

"What art thou weeping for, Ivan Tsarevich?" asked the Gray Wolf.

"My friend, why should I, good youth, not weep? I have formed a heartfelt love for Yelena the Beautiful, and now I must give her to Tsar Afron for the golden-maned steed; and if I yield her not, then Tsar Afron will dishonor me in all lands."

"I have served thee much, Ivan Tsarevich," said the Gray Wolf, "and I will do yet this service. Listen to me. I will turn myself into a princess, Yelena the Beautiful. Do thou give me to Tsar Afron and take from him the golden-maned steed; he will think me the real princess. And when thou art sitting on the steed and riding far away, I will beg of Tsar Afron permission to walk in the open field.

When he lets me go with the maidens and nurses and all the court ladies, and I am with them in the open field, remember me, and I will come to thee."

The Gray Wolf spoke these words, struck the damp earth, and became a princess, Yelena the Beautiful, so that it was not possible in any way to know that the wolf was not the princess. Ivan Tsarevich told Yelena the Beautiful to wait outside the town, and took the Gray Wolf to the palace of Tsar Afron.

When Ivan Tsarevich came with the pretended Yelena the Beautiful, Tsar Afron was greatly delighted in his heart that he had received a treasure which he had long desired. He took the false maiden, and gave Ivan Tsarevich the golden-maned steed.

Ivan Tsarevich mounted the steed and rode out of the town, seated Yelena the Beautiful with him, and rode on, holding his way toward the kingdom of Tsar Dolmat.

The Gray Wolf lived with Tsar Afron a day, a second, and a third, instead of Yelena the Beautiful. On the fourth day he went to Tsar Afron, begging to go out in the open field to walk, to drive away cruel grief and sorrow. Then Tsar Afron said: "Oh, my beautiful princess Yelena, I will do everything for thee; I will let thee go to the open field to walk!" And straightway he commanded the nurses, the maidens, and all the court ladies to go to the open field and walk with the beautiful princess.

Ivan Tsarevich was riding along his road and path with Yelena the Beautiful, talking with her; and he had forgotten about the Gray Wolf, but afterward remembered. "Oh, where is my Gray Wolf?"

All at once, from wherever he came, the wolf stood before Ivan, and said: "Ivan Tsarevich, sit on me, the Gray Wolf, and let the beautiful princess ride on the golden-maned steed."

Ivan Tsarevich sat on the Gray Wolf, and they went toward the kingdom of Tsar Dolmat. Whether they journeyed long or short, when they had come to the kingdom they stopped about three versts from the capital town; and Ivan Tsarevich began to implore: "Listen to me, Gray Wolf, my dear friend. Thou hast shown me many a service, show me the last one now; and the last one is this:

Couldst thou not turn to a golden-maned steed instead of this one? for I do not like to part with this horse."

Suddenly the Gray Wolf struck the damp earth and became a golden-maned steed. Ivan Tsarevich, leaving princess Yelena in the green meadow, sat on the Gray Wolf and went to the palace of Tsar Dolmat. The moment he came, Tsar Dolmat saw that Ivan Tsarevich was riding on the golden-maned steed, and he rejoiced greatly. Straightway he went out of the palace, met the Tsarevich in the broad court, kissed him, took him by the right hand, and led him into the white stone chambers. Tsar Dolmat on the occasion of such joy gave orders for a feast, and they sat at the oaken table at the spread cloth. They ate, they drank, they amused themselves, and rejoiced exactly two days; and on the third day Tsar Dolmat gave Ivan Tsarevich the Fire-bird together with the golden cage. Ivan took the Fire-bird, went outside the town, sat on the golden-maned steed together with Yelena the Beautiful, and went toward his own native place, toward the kingdom of Tsar Vwislav.

Tsar Dolmat the next day thought to take a ride through the open field on his golden-maned steed. He ordered them to saddle him; he sat on the horse, and rode to the open field. The moment he urged the horse, the horse threw Tsar Dolmat off his back, became the Gray Wolf as before, ran off, and came up with Ivan Tsarevich. "Ivan Tsarevich," said he, "sit on me, the Gray Wolf, and let Yelena the Beautiful ride on the golden-maned steed."

Ivan sat on the Gray Wolf, and they went their way. When the Gray Wolf had brought Ivan to the place where he had torn his horse, he stopped and said: "I have served thee sufficiently, with faith and truth. On this spot I tore thy horse in two; to this spot I have brought thee. Come down from me, the Gray Wolf: thou hast a golden-maned steed; sit on him, and go wherever thou hast need. I am no longer thy servant."

The Gray Wolf said these words and ran to one side. Ivan wept bitterly for the Gray Wolf, and went on with the beautiful princess.

Whether he rode long or short with the beautiful princess, when he was within twenty versts of his own kingdom he stopped, dismounted, and he and the beautiful princess rested from the heat of the sun under a tree; he tied the golden-maned steed to the same tree, and put the cage of the Fire-bird by his side. Lying on the soft grass, they talked pleasantly, and fell soundly asleep.

At that time the brothers of Ivan Tsarevich, Dmitri and Vassili Tsarevich, after travelling through many lands without finding the Fire-bird, were on their way home with empty hands, and came unexpectedly upon their brother with the beautiful princess. Seeing the golden-maned steed and the Fire-bird in the cage, they were greatly tempted, and thought of killing their brother Ivan. Dmitri took his own sword out of the scabbard, stabbed Ivan Tsarevich, and cut him to pieces; then he roused the beautiful princess and asked: "Beautiful maiden, of what land art thou, of what father a daughter, and how do they call thee by name?"

The beautiful princess, seeing Ivan Tsarevich dead, was terribly frightened; she began to shed bitter tears, and in her tears she said: "I am Princess Yelena the Beautiful; Ivan Tsarevich, whom ye have given to a cruel death, got me. If ye were good knights, ye would have gone with him into the open field and conquered him there; but ye killed him when asleep; and what fame will ye receive for yourselves? A sleeping man is the same as a dead one."

Then Dmitri Tsarevich put his sword to the heart of Yelena the Beautiful and said: "Hear me, Yelena the Beautiful, thou art now in our hands; we will take thee to our father, Tsar Vwislav, thou wilt tell him that we got thee and the Fire-bird and the golden-maned steed. If not, we will give thee to death this minute." The princess, afraid of death, promised them, and swore by everything sacred that she would speak as commanded. Then they began to cast lots who should have Yelena the Beautiful, and who the golden-maned steed; and the lot fell that the princess should go to Vassili, and the golden-maned steed to Dmitri.

Then Vassili Tsarevich took the princess, and placed her on his horse; Dmitri sat on the golden-maned steed, and took the Fire-bird to give to their father, Tsar Vwislav; and they went their way.

Ivan Tsarevich lay dead on that spot exactly thirty days; then the Gray Wolf ran up, knew Ivan by his odor, wanted to aid him, to bring him to life, but knew not how. Just then the Gray Wolf saw a raven with two young ones who were flying above the body and wanted to eat the flesh of Ivan Tsarevich. The wolf hid behind a bush; and when the young ravens had come down and were ready to eat the body, he sprang out, caught one, and was going to tear it in two. Then the raven came down, sat a little way from the Gray Wolf, and said: "Oh, Gray Wolf, touch not my young child; it has done nothing to thee!"

"Listen to me, raven," said the Gray Wolf. "I will not touch thy child; I will let it go unharmed and well if thou wilt do me a service. Fly beyond the thrice ninth land to the thirtieth kingdom, and bring me the water of death and the water of life."

"I will do that, but touch not my son." Having said these words, the raven flew away and soon disappeared from sight. On the third day the raven returned, bringing two vials, in one the water of life, in the other the water of death, and gave them both to the Gray Wolf. The wolf took the vials, tore the young raven in two, sprinkled it with the water of death; the little raven grew together, he sprinkled it with the water of life, and the raven sprang up and flew away.

The Gray Wolf sprinkled Ivan Tsarevich with the water of death: the body grew together; he sprinkled it with the water of life: Ivan Tsarevich stood up and exclaimed, "Oh, how long I have slept!"

"Thou wouldst have slept forever, had it not been for me. Thy brothers cut thee to pieces and carried off Princess Yelena with the golden-maned steed and the Fire-bird. Now hurry with all speed to thy own country; Vassili Tsarevich will marry thy bride to-day. To reach home quickly, sit on me; I will bear thee."

Ivan sat on the Gray Wolf; the wolf ran with him to the kingdom of Tsar Vwislav, and whether it was long or short, he ran to the edge of the town.

Ivan sprang from the Gray Wolf, walked into the town, and found that his brother Vassili had married Yelena the Beautiful, had returned with her from the ceremony, and was sitting with her at the feast.

Ivan Tsarevich entered the palace; and when Yelena the Beautiful saw him, she sprang up from the table, kissed him, and cried out: "This is my dear bridegroom, Ivan Tsarevich, and not that scoundrel at the table."

Then Tsar Vwislav rose from his place and asked the meaning of these words. Yelena the Beautiful told the whole truth,—told how Ivan Tsarevich had won her, the golden-maned steed, and the Fire-bird; how his elder brother had killed him while asleep; and how they had terrified her into saying that they had won everything.

Tsar Vwislav was terribly enraged at Dmitri and Vassili, and cast them into prison; but Ivan Tsarevich married Yelena the Beautiful, and lived with her in harmony and love, so that one of them could not exist a single minute without the other.

# THE BABA YAGA

Once upon a time there was an old couple. The husband lost his wife and married again. But he had a daughter by the first marriage, a young girl, and she found no favor in the eyes of her evil stepmother, who used to beat her, and consider how she could get her killed outright. One day the father went away somewhere or other, so the stepmother said to the girl, "Go to your aunt, my sister, and ask her for a needle and thread to make you a shift."

Now that aunt was a Baba Yaga. Well, the girl was no fool, so she went to a real aunt of hers first, and says she:

"Good morning, auntie!"

"Good morning, my dear! what have you come for?"

"Mother has sent me to her sister, to ask for a needle and thread to make me a shift."

Then her aunt instructed her what to do. "There is a birch-tree there, niece, which would hit you in the eye—you must tie a ribbon round it; there are doors which would creak and bang—you must pour oil on their hinges; there are dogs which would tear you in pieces—you must throw them these rolls; there is a cat which would scratch your eyes out—you must give it a piece of bacon."

So the girl went away, and walked and walked, till she came to the place. There stood a hut, and in it sat weaving the Baba Yaga, the Bony-shanks.

"Good morning, auntie," says the girl.

"Good morning, my dear," replies the Baba Yaga.

"Mother has sent me to ask you for a needle and thread to make me a shift."

"Very well; sit down and weave a little in the meantime."

So the girl sat down behind the loom, and the Baba Yaga went outside, and said to her servant-maid:

"Go and heat the bath, and get my niece washed; and mind you look sharp after her. I want to breakfast off her."

Well, the girl sat there in such a fright that she was as much dead as alive. Presently she spoke imploringly to the servant-maid, saying:

"Kinswoman dear, do please wet the firewood instead of making it burn; and fetch the water for the bath in a sieve." And she made her a present of a handkerchief.

The Baba Yaga waited awhile; then she came to the window and asked:

"Are you weaving, niece? are you weaving, my dear?"

"Oh yes, dear aunt, I'm weaving." So the Baba Yaga went away again, and the girl gave the Cat a piece of bacon, and asked:

"Is there no way of escaping from here?"

"Here's a comb for you and a towel," said the Cat; "take them, and be off. The Baba Yaga will pursue you, but you must lay your ear on the ground, and when you hear that she is close at hand, first of all throw down the towel. It will become a wide, wide river. And if the Baba Yaga gets across the river, and tries to catch you, then you must lay your ear on the ground again, and when you hear that she is close at hand, throw down the comb. It will become a dense, dense forest; through that she won't be able to force her way anyhow."

The girl took the towel and the comb and fled. The dogs would have rent her, but she threw them the rolls, and they let her go by; the doors would have begun to bang, but she poured oil on their hinges, and they let her pass through; the birch-tree would have poked her eyes out, but she tied the ribbon around it, and it let her pass on. And the Cat sat down to the loom, and worked away; muddled everything about, if it didn't do much weaving. Up came the Baba Yaga to the window, and asked:

"Are you weaving, niece? are you weaving, my dear?"

"I'm weaving, dear aunt, I'm weaving," gruffly replied the Cat.

The Baba Yaga rushed into the hut, saw that the girl was gone, and took to beating the Cat, and abusing it for not having scratched the girl's eyes out. "Long as I've served you," said the Cat, "you've never given me so much as a bone; but she gave me bacon." Then the Baba Yaga pounced upon the dogs, on the doors, on the birch-tree, and on the servant-maid, and set to work to abuse them all, and to knock them about. Then the dogs said to her, "Long as we've served you, you've never so much as pitched us a burnt crust; but she gave us rolls to eat." And the doors said, "Long as we've served you, you've never poured even a drop of water on our hinges; but she poured oil on us." The birch-tree said, "Long as I've served you, you've never tied a single thread round me; but she fastened a ribbon around me." And the servant-maid said, "Long as I've served you, you've never given me so much as a rag; but she gave me a handkerchief."

The Baba Yaga, bony of limb, quickly jumped into her mortar, sent it flying along with the pestle, sweeping away the while all traces of its flight with a broom, and set off in pursuit of the girl. Then the girl put her ear to the ground, and when she heard that the Baba Yaga was chasing her, and was now close at hand, she flung down the towel. And it became a wide, such a wide river! Up came the Baba Yaga to the river, and gnashed her teeth with spite; then she went home for her oxen, and drove them to the river. The oxen drank up every drop of the river, and then the Baba Yaga began the pursuit anew. But the girl put her ear to the ground again, and when she heard that the Baba Yaga was near, she flung down the comb, and instantly a forest sprang up, such an awfully thick one! The Baba Yaga began gnawing away at it, but however hard she worked, she couldn't gnaw her way through it, so she had to go back again.

But by this time the girl's father had returned home, and he asked:

"Where's my daughter?"

"She's gone to her aunt's," replied her stepmother.

Soon afterwards the girl herself came running home.

"Where have you been?" asked her father.

"Ah, father!" she said, "mother sent me to aunt's to ask for a needle and thread to make me a shift. But aunt's a Baba Yaga, and she wanted to eat me!"

"And how did you get away, daughter?"

"Why like this," said the girl, and explained the whole matter. As soon as her father had heard all about it, he became wroth with his wife, and shot her. But he and his daughter lived on and flourished, and everything went well with them.

# THE TSARÉVICH and DYÁD'KA[1]

Once upon a time, in a certain kingdom, in a city of yore, there was a King who had a dwarf son. The Tsarévich was fair to behold, and fair of heart. But his father was not good: he was always tortured with greedy thoughts, how he should derive greater profit from his country and extract heavier taxes.

One day he saw an old peasant passing by with sable, marten, beaver, and fox-skins; and he asked him: "Old man! whence do you come?"

"Out of the village, Father. I serve the Woodsprite with the iron hands, the cast-iron head, and the body of bronze."

"How do you catch so many animals?"

"The Woodsprite lays traps, and the animals are stupid and go into them."

"Listen, old man; I will give you gold and wine. Show me where you put the traps."

So the old man was persuaded, and he showed the King, who instantly had the Woodsprite arrested and confined in a narrow tower. And in all the Woodsprite's forests the King himself laid traps.

The Woodsprite-forester sat in his iron tower inside the royal garden, and looked out through the window. One day, the Tsarévich, with his nurses and attendants and very many faithful servant-maids, went into the garden to play. He

---

1. Affectionate term for old servant, equivalent to uncle.

passed the door, and the Woodsprite cried out to him: "Tsarévich, if you will set me free, I will later on help you."

"How shall I do this?"

"Go to your mother and weep bitterly. Tell her: 'Please, dear Mother, scratch my head.' Lay your head on her lap. Wait for the proper instant, take the key of my tower out of her pocket, and set me free."

Iván Tsarévich did what the Woodsprite had told him, took the key; then he ran into the garden, made an arrow, put the arrow on a catapult, and shot it far away. And all the nurses and serving-maids ran off to find the arrow. Whilst they were all running after the arrow Iván Tsarévich opened the iron tower and freed the Woodsprite. The Woodsprite escaped and destroyed all the King's traps.

Now the King could not catch any more animals, and became angry, and attacked his wife for giving the key away and setting the Woodsprite free. He assembled all the *boyárs*, generals, and senators to pronounce the Queen's doom, whether she should have her head cut off, or should be merely banished. So the Tsarévich was greatly grieved; he was sorry for his mother, and he acknowledged his guilt to his father.

Then the King was very sorry, and didn't know what to do to his son. He asked all the *boyárs* and generals, and said: "Is he to be hanged or to be put into a fortress?"

"No, your Majesty!" the *boyárs*, and generals, and senators answered in one voice. "The scions of kings are not slain, and are not put in prison; they are sent out into the white world to meet whatever fate God may send them."

So Iván Tsarévich was sent out into the white world, to wander in the four directions, to suffer the midday winds and the stress of the winter and the blasts of the autumn; and was given only a birch-bark wallet and Dyád'ka, his servant.

So the King's son set out with his servant into the open fields. They went far and wide over hill and dale. Their way may have been long, and it may have been short; and they at last reached a well. Then the Tsarévich said to his servant, "Go and fetch me water."

"I will not go!" said the servant.

So they went further on, and they once more came to a well.

"Go and fetch me water—I feel thirsty," the Tsarévich asked him a second time. "I will not go."

Then they went on until they came to a third well. And the servant again would not fetch any water. And the Tsarévich had to do it himself. When the Tsarévich had gone down into the well the servant shut down the lid, and said: "You be my servant, and I will be the Tsarévich; or I will never let you come out!"

The Tsarévich could not help himself, and was forced to give way; and signed the bond to his servant in his own blood. Then they changed clothes and rode on, and came to another land, where they went to the Tsar's court, the servant-man first, and the King's son after.

The servant-man sat as a guest with the Tsar, ate and drank at his table. One day he said: "Mighty Tsar, send my servant into the kitchen!"

So they took the Tsarévich as scullion, let him draw water and hew wood. But very soon the Tsarévich was a far finer cook than all the royal chefs. Then the Tsar noticed and began to like his young scullion, and gave him gold. So all the cooks became envious and sought some opportunity of getting rid of the Tsarévich. One day he made a cake and put it into the oven, so the cooks put poison in and spread it over the cake. And the Tsar sat at table, and the cake was taken up. When the Tsar was going to take it, the cook came running up, and cried out: "Your Majesty, do not eat it!" And he told all imaginable lies of Iván Tsarévich. Then the King summoned his favourite hound and gave him a bit of the cake. The dog ate it and died on the spot.

So the Tsar summoned the Prince and cried out to him in a thundering voice: "How dared you bake me a poisoned cake! You shall be instantly tortured to death!"

"I know nothing about it; I had no idea of it, your Majesty!" the Tsarévich answered. "The other cooks were jealous of your rewarding me, and so they have deliberately contrived the plot."

Then the Tsar pardoned him, and he made him a horseherd.

One day, as the Tsarévich was taking his drove to drink, he met the Woodsprite with the iron hands, the cast-iron head, and the body of bronze. "Good-day, Tsarévich; come with me, visit me."

"I am frightened that the horses will run away."

"Fear nothing. Only come."

His hut was quite near. The Woodsprite had three daughters, and he asked the eldest: "What will you give Iván Tsarévich for saving me out of the iron tower?"

"I will give him this table-cloth."

With the table-cloth Iván Tsarévich went back to his horses, which were all gathered together, turned it round and asked for any food that he liked, and he was served, and meat and drink appeared at once.

Next day he was again driving his horses to the river, and the Woodsprite appeared once more. "Come into my hut!"

So he went with him. And the Woodsprite asked his second daughter, "What will you give Iván Tsarévich for saving me out of the iron tower?"

"I will give him this mirror, in which he can see all he will."

And on the third day the third daughter gave him a pipe, which he need only put to his lips, and music, and singers, and musicians would appear before him.

And it was a merry life that Iván Tsarévich now led. He had good food and good meat, knew whatever was going on, saw everything, and he had music all day long: no man was better. And the horses! They—it was really wonderful—were always well fed, well set-up, and shapely.

Now, the fair Tsarévna had been noticing the horseherd for a long time, for a very long time, for how could so fair a maiden overlook the beautiful boy? She wanted to know why the horses he kept were always so much shapelier and statelier than those which the other herds looked after. "I will one day go into his room," she said, "and see where the poor devil lives." As every one knows, a woman's wish is soon her deed. So one day she went into his room, when Iván Tsarévich was giving his horses drink. And there she saw the mirror, and looking into that she knew everything. She took the magical cloth, the mirror, and the pipe.

Just about then there was a great disaster threatening the Tsar. The seven-headed monster, Ídolishche, was invading his land and demanding his daughter as his wife. "If you will not give her to me willy, I will take her nilly!" he said. And he got ready all his immense army, and the Tsar fared ill. And he issued a decree throughout his land, summoned the *boyárs* and knights together, and promised any who would slay the seven-headed monster half of his wealth and half his realm, and also his daughter as his wife.

Then all the princes and knights and the *boyárs* assembled together to fight the monster, and amongst them Dyád'ka. The horseherd sat on a pony and rode behind.

Then the Woodsprite came and met him, and said: "Where are you going, Iván Tsarévich?"

"To the war."

"On this sorry nag you will not do much, and still less if you go in your present guise. Just come and visit me."

He took him into his hut and gave him a glass of *vódka*. Then the King's son drank it. "Do you feel strong?" asked the Woodsprite.

"If there were a log there fifty *puds*, I could throw it up and allow it to fall on my head without feeling the blow."

So he was given a second glass of *vódka*.

"How strong do you feel now?"

"If there were a log here one hundred *puds*, I could throw it higher than the clouds on high."

Then he was given a third glass of *vódka*.

"How strong are you now?"

"If there were a column stretching from heaven to earth, I should turn the entire universe round."

So the Woodsprite took *vódka* out of another bottle and gave the King's son yet more drink, and his strength was increased sevenfold. They went in front of the house; and he whistled loud, and a black horse rose out of the earth, and the earth trembled under its hoofs. Out of its nostrils it breathed flames, columns of smoke rose from its ears, and as its hoofs struck the ground sparks arose. It ran up to the hut and fell on its knees.

"There is a horse!" said the Woodsprite. And he gave Iván Tsarévich a sword and a silken whip.

So Iván Tsarévich rode out on his black steed against the enemy. On the way he met his servant, who had climbed a birch-tree and was trembling for fear. Iván Tsarévich gave him a couple of blows with his whip, and started out against the hostile host. He slew many people with the sword, and yet more did his horse trample down. And he cut off the seven heads of the monster.

Now Marfa Tsarévna was seeing all this, because she kept looking in the glass, and so learned all that was going on. After the battle she rode out to meet Iván Tsarévich, and asked him: "How can I thank you?"

"Give me a kiss, fair maiden!"

The Tsarévna was not ashamed, pressed him to her very heart, and kissed him so loud that the entire host heard it!

Then the King's son struck his horse one blow and vanished. Then he returned to his room, and sat there as though nothing had happened, whilst his servant boasted that he had gone to the battle and slain the foe. So the Tsar awarded him great honours, promised him his daughter, and set a great feast. But the Tsarévna was not so stupid, and said she had a severe headache.

What was the future son-in-law to do? "Father," he said to the Tsar, "give me a ship, I will go and get drugs for my bride; and see that your herdsman comes with me, as I am so well accustomed to him."

The Tsar consented; gave him the ship and the herdsman.

So they sailed away, may be far or near. Then the servant had a sack sewn, and the Prince put into it, and cast him into the water. But the Tsarévna saw the evil thing that had been done, through her magic mirror; and she quickly summoned her carriage and drove to the sea, and on the shore there the Woodsprite sat weaving a great net.

"Woodsprite, help me on my way, for Dyád'ka the servant has drowned the King's son!"

"Here, maiden, look, the net is ready. Help me with your white hands."

Then the Tsarévna threw the net into the deep; fished the King's son up, took him home, and told her father the whole story.

So they celebrated a merry wedding and held a great feast. In a Tsar's palace mead has not to be brewed or any wine to be drawn; there is always enough ready.

Then the servant in the meantime was buying all sorts of drugs, and came back. He came to the palace, was seized, but prayed for mercy. But he was too late, and he was shot in front of the castle gate.

The wedding of the King's son was very jolly, and all the inns and all the beer-houses were opened for an entire week, for everybody, without any charge.

I was there. I drank honey and mead, which came up to my moustache, but never entered my mouth.

# THE SEVEN SIMEONS,
# FULL BROTHERS

Thus lived an old man and his old wife; they lived many years, to a great age. Then they began to pray to God to give them a child who in their old age might help them to work. They prayed a year, they prayed a second, they prayed a third and fourth, they prayed a fifth and a sixth, and did not receive a child; but in the seventh year the Lord gave them seven sons, and they called them all Simeon. When the old man with the old woman died, the Simeons were left orphans all in their tenth year.

They ploughed their own land, and were not worse than their neighbors. It happened one time to Tsar Ador, the ruler of all that country, to pass their village, and he saw the Seven Simeons working in the field. He wondered greatly that such small boys were ploughing and harrowing. Therefore he sent his chief boyar to inquire whose children they were. When the boyar came to the Simeons he asked why they, such small children, were doing such heavy work?

The eldest Simeon answered that they were orphans, that there was no one to work for them, and said at the same time that they were all called Simeon. The boyar left them and told this to the Tsar, who wondered greatly that so many small boys, brothers, should be called by one name. Therefore he sent the same boyar to take them to the palace. The boyar carried out the command of the Tsar and took all the Simeons with him. When the Tsar came to the palace he assembled the *boyárs* and men of counsel and asked advice in the following words:

"My *boyárs* and men of counsel, ye see these seven orphans who have no relatives: I wish to make of them men who may be grateful to me hereafter; therefore I ask counsel of you. In what science or art should I have them instructed?"

To this all answered as follows: "Most Gracious Sovereign, as they are now grown somewhat and have reason, dost thou not think it well to ask each one of them separately with what science or art he would like to occupy himself?"

The Tsar accepted this advice gladly, and began by asking the eldest Simeon: "Listen to me, my friend: with whatever science or art thou wishest to occupy thyself, in that I will have thee instructed."

Simeon answered: "Your Majesty, I have no wish to occupy myself with any science or art; but if you would give command to build a forge in the middle of your court-yard, I would forge a pillar reaching to the sky."

The Tsar saw that there was no reason to teach this Simeon, for he knew well enough the art of a blacksmith; still, he did not believe that the boy could forge a pillar to the very sky, therefore he gave command to build in quick time a forge in the middle of his court-yard. After the first he called the second Simeon. "And thou, my friend, whatever science or art thou wishest to study, in that will I give thee to be taught."

Then that Simeon answered: "Your Majesty, I do not wish to study any science or art; but if my eldest brother will forge a pillar to the sky, then I will climb that pillar to the top, and will look at all lands, and tell you what is going on in each one of them."

The Tsar considered that there was no need to teach this Simeon either, because he was wise already. Then he asked the third Simeon: "Thou, my friend, what science or art dost thou wish to learn?"

Simeon answered: "Your Majesty, I do not wish to learn any science or art; but if my eldest brother will make me an axe, with the axe I will strike once, twice; that moment there will be a ship."

Then the king answered: "I need shipwrights, and thou shouldst not be taught anything else." Next he asked the fourth: "Thou, Simeon, what science or art dost thou wish to know?"

"Your Majesty," answered he, "I do not wish to know any science; but if my third brother should make a ship, and if it should happen to that ship to be at sea, and an enemy should attack it, I would seize it by the prow and take the ship to the underground kingdom; and when the enemy had gone away I would bring it back to the surface of the sea."

The Tsar was astonished at these great wonders of the fourth Simeon, and he said: "There is no need to teach thee either." Then he asked the fifth Simeon: "And thou, Simeon, what science or art dost thou wish to learn?"

"I do not wish to learn any," said he; "but if my eldest brother will make me a gun, with that gun, if I see a bird, I will hit it, even one hundred versts distant."

"Well, thou wilt be a splendid sharpshooter for me," said the Tsar. Then he asked the sixth Simeon: "Thou, Simeon, what science dost thou wish to begin?"

"Your Majesty," said Simeon, "I have no wish to begin any science or art; but if my fifth brother will shoot a bird on the wing, I will not let it reach the earth, but will catch it and bring it to you."

"Thou'rt very cunning," said the Tsar; "thou wilt take the place of a retriever for me in the field." Then the Tsar asked the last Simeon: "What art or science dost thou wish to learn?"

"Your Majesty," answered he, "I do not wish to learn any science or art, because I have a most precious craft."

"But what is thy craft? Tell me, if it please thee."

"I know how to steal dexterously," said Simeon, "so that no man can steal in comparison with me."

The Tsar became greatly enraged, hearing of such an evil art, and said to his *boyárs* and men of counsel: "Gentlemen, how do ye advise me to punish this thief Simeon? Tell me what death should he die?"

"Your Majesty," said they all to him, "why put him to death? He is a thief in name, but a thief who may be needed on an occasion."

"For what reason?" asked the Tsar.

"For this reason: your Majesty is trying now these ten years to get Tsarevna Yelena the Beautiful, and you have not been able to get her; and besides, have lost great forces and armies, and spent much treasure and other things. Mayhap this

Simeon the thief may in some way be able to steal Yelena the Beautiful for your Majesty."

The Tsar said in answer: "My friends, ye tell me the truth." Then he turned to Simeon the thief and asked: "Well, Simeon, canst thou go to the thrice-ninth land, to the thirtieth kingdom, and steal for me Yelena the Beautiful? I am strongly in love with her, and if thou canst steal her for me I'll give thee a great reward."

"Stealing is my art, your Majesty," answered the seventh Simeon, "and I will steal her for you; only give the command."

"Not only do I give the command, but I beg thee to do it; and delay no longer at my court, but take for thyself troops and money, whatever is needed."

"Neither troops nor treasure do I need," answered he. "Let all of us brothers go together, and I will get Tsarevna Yelena the Beautiful."

The Tsar did not like to part with all the Simeons; still, though he regretted it, he was obliged to let them all go together. Meanwhile the forge was built in the court, and the eldest Simeon forged an iron pillar to the very sky; the second Simeon climbed on that pillar to the top, and looked in the direction in which was the kingdom of the father of Yelena the Beautiful. After he had looked he cried from the top of the pillar: "Your Majesty, I see Yelena the Beautiful sitting beyond the thrice-ninth land in the thirtieth kingdom under a window; her marrow flows from bone to bone."

Now the Tsar was still more enticed by her beauty, and said to the Simeons in a loud voice: "My friends, start on your journey at once, for I cannot live without Yelena, the beautiful Tsarevna."

The eldest Simeon made an axe for the third, and for the fifth he made a gun; and after that they took bread for the journey, and Simeon the Thief took a cat, and they went their way. Simeon the Thief had made the cat so used to him that she ran after him everywhere like a dog; and if he stopped on the road, or in any other place, the cat stood on her hind legs, rubbed against him, and purred. So the brothers went their way for some time, and at last came to the sea, which they had to cross, and there was nothing to cross upon. They walked along the shore and looked for a tree of some kind to make a vessel, and they found a very large oak. The third Simeon took his axe and cut the oak at the very root, and then with one stroke and another he made straightway a ship, which was rigged, and in the ship were various costly goods. All the Simeons sat on that ship and sailed on their journey.

In a few months they arrived safely at the place where it was necessary for them to go. When they entered the harbor they cast anchor at once. On the following day Simeon the Thief took his cat and went into the town, and coming to the Tsar's palace he stood opposite the window of Yelena the Beautiful. At that moment the cat stood on her hind legs and began to rub against him and to purr. It is necessary to say that in that kingdom they knew nothing of cats, and had not heard what kind of beast the cat is.

Tsarevna Yelena the Beautiful was sitting at the window; and seeing the cat, sent straightway her nurses and maidens to ask Simeon what kind of beast that was, would he not sell it, and what price would he take. The maidens and nurses ran out in the street and asked Simeon what kind of beast that was, and would he not sell it?

Simeon answered: "My ladies, be pleased to relate to her Highness, Yelena the Beautiful, that this little beast is called a cat, that I will not sell it, but if she wishes to have it I will give it to her without price."

The maidens and nurses ran straight to the palace and told what they had heard from Simeon.

Tsarevna Yelena the Beautiful was rejoiced beyond measure, ran out herself, and asked Simeon would he not sell the cat.

Simeon said: "Your Highness, I will not sell the cat; but if you like her, then I make you a present of her."

The Tsarevna took the cat in her arms and went to the palace, and Simeon she commanded to follow. When she came to the palace the Tsarevna went to her father, and showed him the cat, explaining that a certain foreigner had given it to her as a present.

The Tsar, seeing such a wonderful little beast, was greatly delighted, and gave orders to call Simeon the Thief; and when he came, the Tsar wished to reward him with money for the cat; but as Simeon would not take it, he said: "My friend, live for the time in my house, and meanwhile, in your presence, the cat will become better used to my daughter."

To this Simeon did not agree, and said to the Tsar: "Your Majesty, I could live with great delight in your house if I had not the ship on which I came to your kingdom, and which I cannot commit to any one; but if you command me, I will come every day and teach the cat to know your daughter."

The Tsar commanded Simeon to come every day. Simeon began to visit Tsarevna Yelena the Beautiful. One day he said to her: "Gracious lady, often have I come here; I see that you are not pleased to walk anywhere; you might come to my ship, and I would show you such costly brocades as you have never seen till this day."

The Tsarevna went straightway to her father and began to beg permission to go to the ship-wharf. The Tsar permitted her, and told her to take nurses and maidens, and go with Simeon.

As soon as they came to the wharf Simeon invited her to his ship, and when she entered the ship Simeon and his brothers began to show the Tsarevna various rich brocades. Then Simeon the Thief said to Yelena the Beautiful: "Now be pleased to tell your nurses and maidens to leave the ship, because I wish to show you things so costly that they should not see them."

The Tsarevna commanded her maidens and nurses to leave the ship. As soon as they had gone, Simeon the Thief ordered his brothers in silence to cut off the anchor and go to sea with all sail; meanwhile he showed the Tsarevna rich goods and made her presents of some. About two hours had passed while he was showing the stuffs. At last she said it was time for her to go home, the Tsar her father would expect her to dinner. Then she went out of the cabin and saw that the ship was under sail and land no longer in sight.

She struck herself on the breast, turned into a swan, and flew off. The fifth Simeon took his gun that minute and wounded the swan; the sixth Simeon did not let her fall to the water, but brought her back to the ship, where she became a maiden as before.

The nurses and maidens who were at the wharf, seeing the ship move away from the shore with the Tsarevna, ran straight to the Tsar and told him of

Simeon's deceit. Then the Tsar sent a whole fleet in pursuit. When this fleet coming up was very near the ship of the Simeons, the fourth Simeon seized the prow and conducted the ship to the underground kingdom. When the ship had become entirely invisible, the commanders of the fleet thought it was lost, with the Tsarevna; therefore they returned, and reported to the Tsar that Simeon's ship had gone to the bottom with Yelena the Beautiful.

The Simeons arrived at their own kingdom successfully, delivered Yelena the Beautiful to Tsar Ador, who for such a mighty service of the Simeons gave liberty to them all, and plenty of gold, silver, and precious stones, married Yelena the Beautiful himself, and lived with her many years.

# THE RING with
# TWELVE SCREWS

There lived in a village a son with his mother, and the mother was a very old woman. The son was called Ivan the Fool. They lived in a poor little cottage with one window, and in great poverty. Such was their poverty that besides dry bread they ate almost nothing, and sometimes they had not even the dry bread. The mother would sit and spin, and Ivan the Fool would lie on the stove, roll in the ashes, and never wipe his nose. His mother would say to him time and again: "Ivanushka, thou art sitting there with thy nose unwiped. Why not go somewhere, even to the public-house? Some kind man may come along and take thee to work. Thou wouldst have even a bit of bread, while at home here we have nothing to keep the life in us."

"Very well, I'll go," said Ivan. He rose up and went to the public-house. On the way a man met him.

"Where art thou going, Ivan?"

"I am going to hire out to work."

"Come, work for me; I'll give thee such and such wages, and other things too." Ivan agreed. He went to work.

The man had a dog with whelps; one of the whelps pleased Ivan greatly, and he trained it. A year passed, and the time came to pay wages for the work. The man was giving Ivan money, but he answered: "I need not thy money; give me that whelp of thine that I trained."

The man was glad that he had not to pay money, and gave the whelp.

Ivan went home; and when his mother found what he had done, she began to cry, saying: "All people are people, but thou art a fool; we had nothing to eat, and now there is another life to support."

Ivan the Fool said nothing, sat on the stove with unwiped nose, rolling in the ashes, and the whelp with him. Some time passed; whether it was short or long, his mother said again: "Why art thou sitting there without sense; why not go to the public-house? Some good man may come along and hire thee."

"Very good, I'll go," said the Fool.

He took his dog and started. A man met him on the road.

"Where art thou going, Ivan?"

"To find service," said he; "to hire out."

"Come, work for me."

"Very well," said Ivan.

They agreed, and Ivan went again to work; and that man had a cat with kittens. One of the kittens pleased the Fool, and he trained it. The time came for payment.

Ivan the Fool said to this man: "I need not thy money, but give me that kitten."

"If thou wilt have it," said the man.

Now the Fool went home, and his mother cried more than before. "All people are people, but thou wert born a fool. We had nothing to eat, and now we must support two useless lives!"

It was bitter for Ivan to hear this. He took his dog and cat and went out into the field. He saw in the middle of the field a fire burning in a great pile of wood,—such an awful pile of wood! When he drew nearer he saw that a snake was squirming in it, burning on hot coals.

The snake screamed to him in a human voice: "Oh, Ivan the Fool, save me! I will give thee a great ransom for my life."

Ivan took a stick and raised the snake out of the fire.

When he had thrown it out, there stood before him, not a snake, but a beautiful maiden; and she said: "Thanks to thee, Ivanushka. Thou hast done me great service; I will do thee still greater. We will go," said she, "to my mother. She will offer thee copper money: do not take it, because it is coals, and not money; she will offer thee silver coin: do not take that either, for that will be chips, and not silver; she will bring out to thee gold: take not even that, because instead of gold it is potsherds and broken bricks. But ask of her in reward the ring with twelve screws. It will be hard for her to give it; but be firm, she will give it for my sake."

Behold, all took place as she said. Though the old woman grew very angry, she gave the ring. Ivan was going along through the field, thinking, "What shall I do with this ring?"

He was looking at it, when that same young girl caught up with him and said: "Ivan, whatever thou wishest, thou wilt have. Only stand in the evening on the threshold, loosen all the twelve screws, and before thee twelve thousand men will appear: whatever thou wishest, command; all will be done."

Ivan went home, said nothing to his mother, sat on the stove, lay in the ashes with unwiped nose. Evening came; they lay down to sleep.

Ivan waited for the hour, went on the threshold, unscrewed the twelve screws, and twelve thousand men stood before him. "Thou art our master, we are thy men: declare thy soul's desire."

Said Ivan to the men: "Have it made that on this very spot a castle shall stand such as there is not in the world, and that I sleep on a bedstead of gold, on down of swans, and that my mother sleep in like manner; that coachmen, outriders, servants, and all kinds of powerful people be walking in my court and serving me."

"Lie down for thyself in God's name," said the men; "all will be done at thy word."

Ivan the Fool woke up next morning, and was frightened even himself. He looked around; he was sleeping on a golden bedstead on down of swans, and there were lofty chambers and so rich that even the Tsar had not such. In the court-yard were walking coachmen, outriders, servants, and all kinds of mighty and important people who were serving him. The Fool was amazed, and thought, "This is good." He looked in the mirror, and did not know his own self; he had become a beauty that could not be described with a pen or be told of in a tale. As was fitting, the lord was as fine as his chambers.

When the Tsar woke up at the same hour,—and the Tsar lived in that town,— he looked, and behold opposite his palace stood a castle just gleaming in gold.

The Tsar sent to learn whose it was. "Let the owner come to me," said he, "and show what sort of man he is."

They informed Ivan, and he said: "Tell him that this is the castle of Ivan Tsarevich; and if he wants to see me, he is not so great a lord, let him come himself."

There was no help for it. The Tsar had to go to Ivan the Fool's castle. They became acquainted, and after that Ivan the Fool went to the Tsar. The Tsar had a most beautiful young Tsarevna of a daughter, and she brought refreshments to Ivan; and right there she pleased him greatly, and straightway he begged the Tsar to give her in marriage to him. Now the Tsar in his turn began to put on airs.

"Give her,—why not give her? But thou, Ivan Tsarevich, perform a service for me. My daughter is not of common stock, and therefore she must marry only the very best among the whole people. Arrange this for me, that from thy castle to mine there be a golden road, and that I have a bridge over the river,—not a common one, but such a bridge that one side shall be of gold, and the other of silver; and let all kinds of rare birds be swimming on the river,—geese and swans; and on the other side of the river let there be a church,—not a simple one, but one all wax,—and let there grow around it wax apple-trees and bear ripe apples. If thou do this, my daughter shall be thine; and if not, blame thyself." ("Well," thought the Tsar, "I have joked enough with Ivan Tsarevich;" but he kept his own counsel.)

"Agreed," said Ivan. "Now do thou make ready the wedding to-morrow." With that he departed.

In the evening, when all had lain down to sleep, he stood on the threshold, unscrewed all the screws in the ring: twelve thousand men stood before him.

"Thou art our master, we are thy men: command what thy soul desires."

"Thus and thus," said he; "I want this and that."

"All right," said they; "lie down with God."

In the morning the Tsar woke up, went to the window; but his eyes were dazzled. He sprang back six paces. That meant that the bridge was there, one side silver, the other gold, just blazing and shining. On the river were geese and swans and every rare bird. On the opposite bank stood a church of white wax, and around the church apple-trees, but without leaves; the naked branches were sticking up.

"Well," thought the Tsar, "the trick has failed; we must prepare our daughter for the wedding."

They arrayed her and drove to the church. When they were driving from the palace, buds began to come out on the apple-trees; when they were crossing the bridge, the apple-trees were coming into leaf; when they were driving up to the church, white blossoms were bursting forth on the trees; and when the time came to go home from the marriage ceremony, the servants and all kinds of people met them, gave them ripe apples on a golden salver. Then they began to celebrate the wedding. Feasts and balls were given; they had a feast which lasted three days and three nights.

After that, whether it was a short time or a long one, the Tsarevna began to tease Ivan. "Tell me, my dear husband, how dost thou do all this? How dost thou build a bridge in one night, and a wax church?"

Ivan the Fool would not tell her for a long time; but as he loved her very much, and she begged very hard, he said: "I have a ring with twelve screws, and it must be handled in such and such fashion."

Well, they lived on. The misery of the matter was this: one of their servants pleased the Tsarevna,—he was a fine-looking, shapely, strong fellow, and she conspired with him to rob her husband, take away the ring, and the two would then go to live beyond the sea.

As soon as evening came she took out the ring quietly, stood on the threshold, and unscrewed the twelve screws: twelve thousand men stood before her.

"Thou art our mistress, we are thy men: command what thy soul desires."

She said: "Take this castle for me and bear it beyond the sea, with all that is in it; and on this spot let the old cabin stand, with my ragged husband, Ivan the Fool, inside."

"Lie down with God," said the men; "all will be done on thy word."

Next morning Ivan woke up, looked around. He was lying on a bark mat, covered with a ragged coat, and not a sign of his castle. He began to cry bitterly, and went to the Tsar, his father-in-law. He came to the palace, asked to announce to the Tsar that his son-in-law had come. When the Tsar saw him he said: "Oh, thou this and that kind of breechesless fellow, what son-in-law art thou to me?

My sons-in-law live in golden chambers and ride in silver carriages. Take him and wall him up in a stone pillar."

It was commanded and done. They took Ivan and walled him up in a stone pillar. But the cat and the dog did not leave him, they were there too, and dug out a hole for themselves; through the hole they gave food to Ivan. But one time they thought: "Why do we sit here, dog and cat, with folded hands? Let's run beyond the sea and get the ring."

As they decided to do that, they did it. They swam through the sea, found their castle. The Tsarevna was walking in the garden with the servant, laughing at her husband.

"Well, do thou remain here a while, and I'll go to the chamber and get the ring," said the cat; and she went her way, mi-au, mi-au, under the door. The Tsarevna heard her, and said: "Ah, here is that scoundrel's cat; let her in and feed her." They let her in and fed her. The cat walked through the chambers all the time and looked for the ring. She saw on the stove a glass box, and in the box the ring.

The cat was delighted. "Glory be to God!" thought she. "Now only wait for night; I'll get the ring, and then for home!"

When all had lain down, the cat sprang on to the stove and threw down the glass box; it fell, and was broken. She caught the ring in her mouth and hid under the door. All in the house were roused; the Tsarevna herself got up, and saw that the box was broken.

"Oh!" said she, "it must be the cat of that scoundrel broke it. Drive her out; drive her out!"

They chased out the cat, and she was glad; she ran to the dog.

"Well, brother dog," said she, "I have the ring. Now if we could only get home quickly!"

They swam through the sea, were a long time swimming. When the dog was tired, he sat on the cat; when the cat was tired, she sat on the dog; and so they worked on and it was not far from land. But the dog was growing weak. The cat saw this, and said, "Sit thou on me; thou art tired." The minute she said this the ring fell out of her mouth into the water. What was to be done? They swam to shore and wept tears. Meanwhile they grew hungry. The dog ran through the field and caught sparrows for himself, and the cat ran along the shore catching little fish thrown up by the waves; that was how she fed herself.

But all at once the cat cried out: "Oh, thou dog, come here quickly to me; I have found the ring! I caught a fish, began to eat it, and in the fish was the ring."

Now they were both powerfully glad; they ran to Ivan and brought him the ring.

Ivan waited till evening, unscrewed all the twelve screws, and twelve thousand men stood before him.

"Thou art our master, we are thy men: tell us to do what thy soul desires."

"Break in a minute this stone pillar so that dust from it shall not remain; and from beyond the sea bring hither my castle with all who are in it, and every one as sleeping now, and put it in the old place."

Straightway all this was done. In the morning Ivan went to his father-in-law. The Tsar met him, seated him in the first place, and said: "Where hast thou been pleased to pass thy time, my dear son-in-law?"

"I was beyond the sea," said Ivan.

"That's it," said the Tsar, "beyond the sea. 'Tis clear that thou hadst pressing business, for thou didst not come to take farewell of thy father-in-law. But while thou wert gone, some sort of bare-legged fellow came to me and called himself my son-in-law. I gave command to wall him up in a stone pillar; he has perished there, doubtless. Well, beloved son-in-law, where hast thou been pleased to spend thy time; what sights hast thou seen?"

"I have seen," said Ivan, "various sights; and beyond the sea there was an affair of such kind that no man knew how to settle it."

"What was the affair?"

"Well, this is the kind of affair it was; and if thou art a wise man, decide it according to thy wisdom of Tsar: A husband had a wife, and while he was living she found a sweetheart for herself; she robbed her husband, and went away with the sweetheart beyond the sea; and now she is with that man. What, to thy thinking, should be done with that wife?"

"According to my wisdom of Tsar I will utter the following sentence: Tie them both to the tails of horses, and let the horses loose in the open field,—let that be their punishment."

"If that is thy judgment, very well," said Ivan. "Come with me as a guest; I will show thee other sights and another wonder."

They went to Ivan's castle, and found there the Tsar's daughter and the servant. As Ivan had commanded, they were still asleep.

There was no help for it; according to the word of the Tsar they tied them both to the tails of horses and urged the horses into the open field,—that was their punishment. But Ivan afterwards married that beautiful, most beautiful maiden whom he had saved from the fire, and they began to live and win wealth.

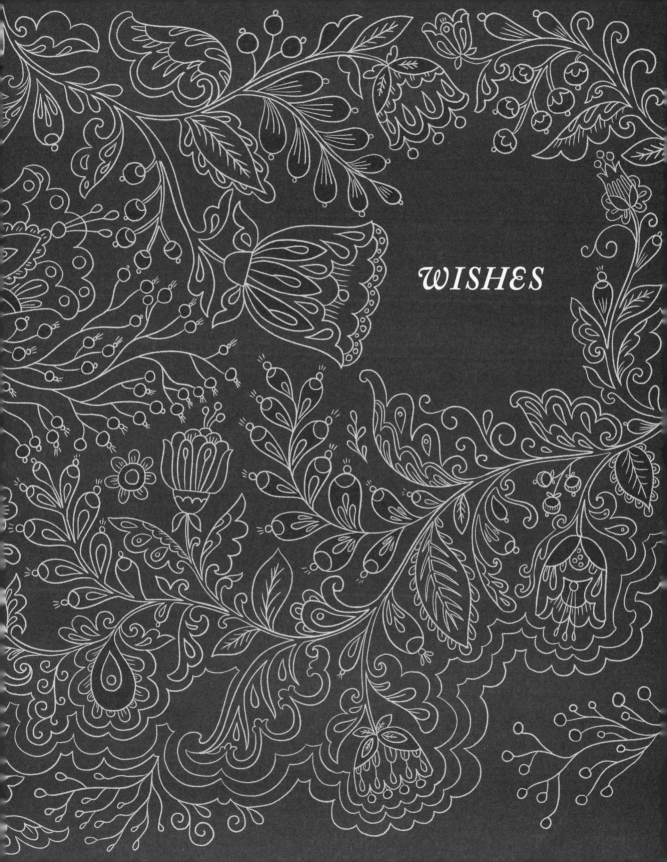

WISHES

# THE SNOW-CHILD

I n a certain village lived a peasant named Ivan, and his wife Mary. They were very fond of each other, and had lived happily together for many years, but unfortunately they had no children. The poor people were sad on that account. Their hearts, however, were gladdened at the sight of their neighbours' children. What could be done? It was evidently the will of Heaven; and in this world, Heaven's will be done!

One day, in winter, after a great quantity of snow had fallen on the ground, the children of the village where Ivan and Mary lived ran into the fields to play. The old couple looked at them from the window. The children ran about, played all sorts of frolics together, and at last began to make a snow-man. Ivan and Mary sat down quietly watching them. Suddenly Ivan smiled and said,—

"I say, wife, let us go out and make a snow-man too."

Mary was also in a merry mood.

"Yes," she answered; "let us go out and play, though we are old. But why should we make a snow-man? Better to make a snow-child, since Heaven will not grant us a live one."

"Very good," said Ivan.

He put on his cap, and went with his wife into the garden.

They really set about making a baby of snow. They made the body; then arms and legs; then put on the top a ball of snow for a head.

"Heaven help you!" cried one who passed by.

"Many thanks," replied Ivan.

"Heaven's help is always acceptable," added Mary.

"What are you doing?" continued the stranger.

"What you yourself see," answered Ivan.

"We are making a Snyegurka!"[1] cried Mary, laughing.

Then they made a little nose and a chin, two little holes for eyes, and as soon as Ivan had finished—oh, wonderful!—a sweet breath came out of its mouth! Ivan lifted up his arms and stared. The little holes were no longer holes; in their place were two bright blue eyes, and the tiny lips smiled lovingly upon him.

"Mercy on us! What is this?" cried Ivan, devoutly crossing himself.

The snow-child turned its head towards him—it was really alive! It moved its arms and legs inside the snow, like an infant in swaddling clothes.

"Oh, Ivan," cried Mary, trembling with joy, "Heaven has at last given us a baby!" and she seized the child in her arms.

The snow fell off "Snyegurka," as Mary called her, like the shell from a chicken. Mary, delighted beyond measure, held in her arms a beautiful, living girl.

"Oh, my love! my love! My darling Snyegurka!" cried the kind-hearted woman, tenderly embracing her long-wished for, and now unexpectedly granted child. Then she rushed into the hut with the infant in her arms. Ivan was astounded at this wonderful event; as to Mary, she was beside herself with joy.

Snyegurka grew every hour; each day she looked more beautiful than before. Ivan and Mary were delighted with her, and their hut, once so quiet and lonely, was now full of life and merriment. The girls of the village visited them constantly; dressed and played with Snyegurka as if she were a doll; talked to her; sang songs to her; joined her with them in all their games, and taught her all they knew themselves. Snyegurka was very clever, and quickly learnt everything she was told. During the winter she grew up as tall as a girl of thirteen years old; she understood and could talk about most things around her, and had such a sweet voice that one would never tire of listening to it. Besides this, she was kind, obedient, and affectionate. Her flesh was as white as snow; her eyes looked like two forget-me-nots; and her hair was of a light flaxen colour. Her cheeks only had no rosy hue in

---

1. Snow-child

them, because there was no blood in her veins. In spite of this she was so beautiful, that, having once seen her, you would wish to see her again and again. It would have done your heart good to see how she enjoyed herself, and how happy she was when at play. Everybody loved her; she was idolised by Mary, who would often say to her husband, "Heaven has granted us joy in our old age; sorrow has left my heart!"

Ivan would answer, "Heaven be praised! But in this world happiness is seldom lasting, and sorrow is good for us all."

The long winter had gradually glided away. The glorious sun again shone in the sky, and warmed the cold earth. Where the snow melted, green grass appeared, and the skylark poured forth its sweet notes. The girls of the village collected together, and welcomed the spring with a song:—

"Beautiful Spring! How did you come to us? How did you make your journey? On a plough or on a harrow?"[2]

From a gay, sprightly girl, Snyegurka suddenly became sad.

"What is the matter with you, my dearest child?" Mary would often ask, drawing Snyegurka nearer to her heart. "Are you ill? You are not so happy as you used to be. Perhaps an evil eye has glanced at you?"

Snyegurka would simply answer, "I am well; mother."

The snow had now completely melted away, and the genial spring appeared with its warm and sunny days. The meadows and gardens began to be covered with radiant and sweet-scented flowers. The nightingale and other songsters of the woods and fields resumed their beautiful melodies. In a word, all nature became brighter and more charming.

Snyegurka alone grew sadder and sadder. She began to shun her playfellows, and to hide herself from the rays of the sun like the May-flower under the tree. She would only play near a well of spring water—splashing and dabbling in it with her hand—beneath the shade of a green willow. She grew daily fonder of the shade, the cool air, and the rain shower. During rain, and in the evening, she would become more gay. When the sky became overcast with dark clouds, and a thick shower of hail came pouring down, Snyegurka was as pleased as any other

---

2. It is customary in some Slavonic countries to welcome the appearance of spring with song.

girl would have been at the sight of a pearl necklace. When the hail melted and disappeared beneath the warm rays of the sun, Snyegurka cried bitterly, as if she herself would melt into tears; as an affectionate sister might weep over a lost brother.

The spring now ended, the summer came, and the Feast of St. John was close at hand. All the girls from the village went into the wood to play. Several of them came to the hut, and asked Mistress Mary to allow Snyegurka to go with them. Mary was at first afraid to let Snyegurka go, and the girl herself did not care about it, but they could not very well refuse the invitation. Then Mary thought it would perhaps amuse Snyegurka. She therefore kissed her tenderly, saying,—

"Go, my dear child; go and enjoy yourself. And you, my good girls, take care of my Snyegurka. You know she is as dear to me as my very sight."

"All right! we'll take care!" cried the girls; and they caught hold of Snyegurka by the arms, and ran away together to the forest.

There they made garlands and bouquets of flowers, and sang songs, while Snyegurka took part in their play.

After sunset the girls piled up a small heap of dry grass and brushwood, lighted it, and, with garlands on their heads, stood in a line, one close upon the other. They put Snyegurka at the end, and said, "When you see us running, you run after us." Then they began to sing, and to jump over the fire.

Suddenly they heard a painful cry. They turned round quickly, but could see nothing. Greatly surprised, they looked at each other, and then noticed that Snyegurka was missing. "Oh, the mischievous puss!" cried the girls; "she has hidden herself."

They ran in every direction in search of her, but all in vain. They called her by her name, "Snyegurka!" but there was no answer.

"Perhaps she has gone home," cried some of the girls. They all ran back to the village—Snyegurka was not there!

They searched for her the whole night, the following, and the third day; they examined the forest,—every tree, every bush; but all to no purpose, Snyegurka was gone!

Old Ivan and Mary were almost broken-hearted at the loss of their beloved Snyegurka. Every day Mary went to the forest to look for her lost child. Poor woman! like a tender mother full of grief and yearning for her young one, she cried aloud,—

"Ah, me! my Snyegurka! Ah, me! my darling dove! Where art thou?"

She often fancied she could hear her dear Snyegurka's painful cry when she disappeared. Alas! alas! Snyegurka was nowhere to be found.

Where had Snyegurka gone? Had some wild beast seized and dragged her into his lair? or a bird of prey carried her across the dark blue sea to its nest? No; neither bird nor beast had carried the girl away. When Snyegurka, following her companions, sprang over the fire, she melted away and changed in an instant into a beautiful white cloud, rose up, and disappeared in the sky for ever!

# SORROW

Once upon a time, in a wretched village, there lived two peasants, who were own brothers. One was poor, however, and the other rich. The rich man settled in the town, built himself a fine house, and became a merchant. Sometimes the poor brother had not a crumb of bread and the children (each of whom was smaller than the others) cried and begged for something to eat. From morning to evening the peasant trudged away like a fish on ice, but it was all of no good.

One day he said to his wife: "I am going into the town, in order to beg my brother to help me."

So he came to the rich man and asked him: "Brother, help me in my sorrow, for my wife and children sit at home without any bread and are starving."

"If you will work for me this week I will help you."

What was the poor fellow to do? He set to work, cleaned out the courtyard, groomed the horses, carried the water, hewed the wood. When the week had gone by the rich man gave him a loaf of bread. "There, you have a reward for your pains."

"I thank you for it," said the poor man, and bowed down, and was going home.

"Stay," the rich brother said to him: "Come with your wife to-morrow and be my guests. To-morrow is my name-day."

"Oh, brother, how can I? As you know, merchants who wear boots and furs come to see you, whilst I have only bast shoes, and I only have my grey coat."

"Never mind! Come to-morrow; I shall still have room for you."

"Good brother! I will come."

So the poor man went home, gave his wife the loaf of bread, and said: "Listen, wife. To-morrow you and I are to be guests."

"Who has asked us?"

"My brother. To-morrow is his name-day."

"All right, let's go."

Next day they got up and went into the town. They came to the rich man's door, greeted him, and sat down on a bench. And at table there were many guests, and the master of the house entertained them all magnificently. Only he forgot the poor brother and his wife, and he gave them nothing. They sat there, and could only look at the others eating and drinking. When the meal was over the guests rose from table and bowed their thanks to the master and mistress, and the poor man also stood up from his bench and bowed down deep before his brother; and the guests went home drunken and merry, noisily singing songs.

But the poor man went home with an empty stomach. "We too must sing a song!" he said to his wife.

"Oh, you fool, the others sing, for they have had a good dinner and have drunk well. Why should we sing?"

"Well, after all, I was a guest at my brother's name-day, and I am ashamed of going back so silently. If I sing they will all think, anyhow, that I have been served as well."

"Sing if you will! I shall not!"

So the peasant sang and sang, and he heard two voices. So he stopped and asked his wife: "Are you helping me; to sing with a thin voice?"

"What are you thinking of? I was doing nothing of the sort."

"What was it, then?"

"I don't know," said the wife. "Sing. I will listen." So he went on singing by himself, and again the two voices were heard. So he stayed still, and said, "Sorrow, are you aiding me to sing?"

And Sorrow answered: "Yes, I am aiding you."

"Now, Sorrow, we will go on together."

"Yes, I will ever remain with you."

So the peasant went home. But Sorrow called him into the inn.

He said: "I have no money."

"Never mind, Hodge; what do you want money for? Why, you still have half of a fur; what is the use of it? It will soon be summer, and you will be no longer requiring it. We will go into the inn and drink it up."

So the peasant and Sorrow went into the inn, and they drank up the half-fur. Next day Sorrow groaned and said he had a headache, a fearful headache, owing to last night's treat. And he enticed the peasant once more to bib wine.

"But I have no money!"

"There is no need of money. Take your sleigh and your carriage; that will be sufficient for us!"

It was not any good. The peasant could not escape Sorrow. So he took his sleigh and his carriage, drove them to the inn, and drank them with Sorrow. And in the morning Sorrow groaned yet further, and reduced the master to further drinking; and the peasant drank away his ploughshare and his plough.

One month had gone by, and he had drunk all his property away, pledged his *izbá*[1] to a neighbour, and spent all the money in the inn. Then Sorrow came to him once more. "Let us go to the inn!"

"No, Sorrow, I have no more."

"Why, your wife has two sarafáns, one will be sufficient for her."

So the peasant took the sarafán, drank it up; and he thought: "Now I have not anything left, neither house, nor clothes, nor anything else for myself or my wife!"

Next morning Sorrow woke up and saw that there was nothing more he could take. So he said: "Master, what is your wish? Go to your neighbour and borrow a pair of oxen and a carriage."

So the peasant went to his neighbour and said, "Can you lend me a car and a pair of oxen for a short time, and I will do a week's work for them?"

"What do you want with them?"

"To fetch wood out of the forest."

"Well, then, take them, but don't overload them."

---

1. Hut.

"Oh, of course not, uncle!"

So the peasant took the oxen, went with Sorrow into the carriage, and drove into the field.

"Do you know the big stone in this field?" Sorrow asked.

"Oh, yes!"

"Well, then, drive up to it."

So they arrived at the stone and dismounted. Sorrow bade the peasant lift up the stone, and he aided him in the work. Under the stone there was a hollow filled with gold.

"Now, what do you see?" said Sorrow. "Load it all up quickly on to the coach."

So the peasant set to work sharply, loaded all the gold up, to the very last ducats. And when he noticed there was not anything left, he said, "Sorrow, is there no more gold there?"

"I don't see any."

"Down there in the corner I see something glittering."

"No; I cannot see anything."

"Get down into the pit, and you will see it."

So Sorrow went into the pit, and as soon as he was in the peasant cast the stone in. "Things will now go better," said the peasant, "for if I were to take you back with me, Sorrow, you would drink up all of this money!"

So the peasant went home, and he poured out the gold in the cellar. He took the oxen back to his neighbour, and he began to set up house again, bought a wood, built a big house, and became twice as rich as his brother. Soon he rode to the town, in order to invite his brother and his sister-in-law to his own name-day.

"Whatever do you mean?" said the rich brother, "why, you have nothing to eat, and you are giving festivals!"

"I had nothing to eat before, but I am now as well off as you are."

"All right; I will come."

So next day the rich man, with his wife, went to the name-day; and they saw that the poor starveling had a big new house, much finer than many merchants' houses. And the peasant gave them a rich dinner, with all kinds of meat and drink.

So the rich man asked his brother: "Tell me, how did you become so rich?"

Then the peasant told him the bare truth—how Sorrow had followed on his heels and how he and his Sorrow had gone into the inn, and he had drunk away all his goods and chattels to the last shred, until he had only his soul left in his body; and then how Sorrow had showed him the treasure-trove in the field, and he had thus freed himself from the thraldom of Sorrow.

And the rich man became envious and thought: "I will go into the field and will lift the stone up. Sorrow will rend my brother's body asunder, so that he cannot then brag of his riches in front of me."

So he left his wife behind and drove into the field, to the big stone. He whirled it off to the side and bowed down to see what was under the stone. And he had hardly bowed down, when Sorrow sprang up and sat on his shoulders.

"O!" Sorrow cried. "You wanted to leave me here under the earth. Now I shall never depart from you."

"Listen, Sorrow: I was not the person who locked you up here!"

"Who was it, then, if it was not you?"

"My brother. I came in order to set you free."

"No, you are lying and deceiving me again. This time it shall not come off."

So Sorrow sat fast on the wretched merchant's shoulders. He brought Sorrow with him home, and his household went from bad to worse. Sorrow began early in the morning enticing the merchant into the beerhouse day after day, and much property was drunk away.

"This life is absolutely unbearable!" thought the merchant. "I have done Sorrow too good a service. I must now set myself free from him. How shall I?" So he thought and he thought it out. He went into his courtyard, cut two oak wedges, took a new wheel, and knocked one wedge from one end into the axle. He went up to Sorrow. "Now, Sorrow, must you lie about like that?"

"What should I be doing? What else is there to do?"

"Come into the courtyard; let us play hide-and-seek."

This suited Sorrow down to the ground, and at first the merchant hid and Sorrow found him at once.

Then Sorrow had to hide. "You will not find me so easily: I can hide myself in any crack."

"What!" said the merchant. "Why, you could never get into this wheel, much less into a crack!"

"What! I could not get into the wheel? Just look how I manage to hide myself in it!"

So Sorrow crept into the wheel, and the merchant took the other oak wedge and drove it into the hub from the other side, and threw the wheel, with Sorrow inside, into the river. Sorrow was drowned, and the merchant lived as before.

# WEDNESDAY

A young housewife was spinning late one evening. It was during the night between a Tuesday and a Wednesday. She had been left alone for a long time, and after midnight, when the first cock crew, she began to think about going to bed, only she would have liked to finish spinning what she had in hand. "Well," thinks she, "I'll get up a bit earlier in the morning, but just now I want to go to sleep." So she laid down her hatchel—but without crossing herself—and said:

"Now then, Mother Wednesday, lend me thy aid, that I may get up early in the morning and finish my spinning." And then she went to sleep.

Well, very early in the morning, long before it was light, she heard someone moving, bustling about the room. She opened her eyes and looked. The room was lighted up. A splinter of fir was burning in the cresset, and the fire was lighted in the stove. A woman, no longer young, wearing a white towel by way of head-dress, was moving about the cottage, going to and fro, supplying the stove with firewood, getting everything ready. Presently she came up to the young woman, and roused her, saying, "Get up!" The young woman got up, full of wonder, saying:

"But who art thou? What hast thou come here for?"

"I am she on whom thou didst call. I have come to thy aid."

"But who art thou? On whom did I call?"

"I am Wednesday. On Wednesday surely thou didst call. See, I have spun thy linen and woven thy web: now let us bleach it and set it in the oven. The oven is heated and the irons are ready; do thou go down to the brook and draw water."

The woman was frightened, and thought: "What manner of thing is this?" but Wednesday glared at her angrily; her eyes just did sparkle!

So the woman took a couple of pails and went for water. As soon as she was outside the door she thought: "Mayn't something terrible happen to me? I'd better go to my neighbor's instead of fetching the water." So she set off. The night was dark. In the village all were still asleep. She reached a neighbor's house, and rapped away at the window until at last she made herself heard. An aged woman let her in.

"Why, child!" says the old crone; "whatever hast thou got up so early for? What's the matter?"

"Oh, granny, this is how it was. Wednesday has come to me, and has sent me for water to buck my linen with."

"That doesn't look well," says the old crone. "On that linen she will either strangle thee or scald thee."

The old woman was evidently well acquainted with Wednesday's ways.

"What am I to do?" says the young woman. "How can I escape from this danger?"

"Well, this is what thou must do. Go and beat thy pails together in front of the house, and cry, 'Wednesday's children have been burnt at sea!' She will run out of the house, and do thou be sure to seize the opportunity to get into it before she comes back, and immediately slam the door to, and make the sign of the cross over it. Then don't let her in, however much she may threaten you or implore you, but sign a cross with your hands, and draw one with a piece of chalk, and utter a prayer. The Unclean Spirit will have to disappear."

Well, the young woman ran home, beat the pails together, and cried out beneath the window:

"Wednesday's children have been burnt at sea!"

Wednesday rushed out of the house and ran to look, and the woman sprang inside, shut the door, and set a cross upon it. Wednesday came running back, and began crying: "Let me in, my dear! I have spun thy linen; now will I bleach it." But the woman would not listen to her, so Wednesday went on knocking at the door until cock-crow. As soon as the cocks crew, she uttered a shrill cry and disappeared. But the linen remained where it was.

# FROST

There was once an old man who had a wife and three daughters. The wife had no love for the eldest of the three, who was her stepdaughter, but was always scolding her. Moreover, she used to make her get up ever so early in the morning, and gave her all the work of the house to do. Before daybreak the girl would feed the cattle and give them to drink, fetch wood and water indoors, light the fire in the stove, give the room a wash, mend the dresses, and set everything in order. Even then her stepmother was never satisfied, but would grumble away at Marfa, exclaiming:—

"What a lazybones! what a slut! Why here's a brush not in its place, and there's something put wrong, and she's left the muck inside the house!"

The girl held her peace, and wept; she tried in every way to accommodate herself to her stepmother, and to be of service to her stepsisters. But they, taking pattern by their mother, were always insulting Marfa, quarrelling with her, and making her cry: that was even a pleasure to them! As for them, they lay in bed late, washed themselves in water got ready for them, dried themselves with a clean towel, and didn't sit down to work till after dinner.

Well, our girls grew and grew, until they grew up and were old enough to be married. The old man felt sorry for his eldest daughter, whom he loved because she was industrious and obedient, never was obstinate, always did as she was bid, and never uttered a word of contradiction. But he didn't know how he was to help her in her trouble. He was feeble, his wife was a scold, and her daughters were as obstinate as they were indolent.

Well, the old folks set to work to consider—the husband how he could get his daughters settled, the wife how she could get rid of the eldest one. One day she says to him:—

"I say, old man! let's get Marfa married."

"Gladly," says he, slinking off (to the sleeping-place) above the stove. But his wife called after him:—

"Get up early to-morrow, old man, harness the mare to the sledge, and drive away with Marfa. And, Marfa, get your things together in a basket, and put on a clean shift; you're going away to-morrow on a visit."

Poor Marfa was delighted to hear of such a piece of good luck as being invited on a visit, and she slept comfortably all night. Early next morning she got up, washed herself, prayed to God, got all her things together, packed them away in proper order, dressed herself (in her best things), and looked something like a lass!—a bride fit for any place whatsoever!

Now it was winter time, and out of doors was a rattling frost. Early in the morning, between daybreak and sunrise, the old man harnessed the mare to the sledge, and led it up to the steps. Then he went indoors, sat down on the window-sill, and said:—

"Now then! I've got everything ready."

"Sit down to table and swallow your victuals!" replied the old woman.

The old man sat down to table, and made his daughter sit by his side. On the table stood a pannier; he took out a loaf, and cut bread for himself and his daughter. Meantime his wife served up a dish of old cabbage soup, and said:—

"There, my pigeon, eat and be off; I've looked at you quite enough! Drive Marfa to her bridegroom, old man. And look here, old greybeard! drive straight along the road at first, and then turn off from the road to the right, you know, into the forest—right up to the big pine that stands on the hill, and there hand Marfa over to Morozko (Frost)."

The old man opened his eyes wide, also his mouth, and stopped eating, and the girl began lamenting.

"Now then, what are you hanging your chaps and squealing about?" said her stepmother. "Surely your bridegroom is a beauty, and he's that rich! Why, just see what a lot of things belong to him, the firs, the pine-tops, and the birches, all in their robes of down—ways and means that any one might envy; and he himself a *bogatir!*"

The old man silently placed the things on the sledge, made his daughter put on a warm pelisse, and set off on the journey. After a time, he reached the forest, turned off from the road; and drove across the frozen snow. When he got into the depths of the forest, he stopped, made his daughter get out, laid her basket under the tall pine, and said:—

"Sit here, and await the bridegroom. And mind you receive him as pleasantly as you can."

Then he turned his horse round and drove off homewards.

The girl sat and shivered. The cold had pierced her through. She would fain have cried aloud, but she had not strength enough; only her teeth chattered. Suddenly she heard a sound. Not far off, Frost was cracking away on a fir. From fir to fir was he leaping, and snapping his fingers. Presently he appeared on that very pine under which the maiden was sitting and from above her head he cried:—

"Art thou warm, maiden?"

"Warm, warm am I, dear Father Frost," she replied.

Frost began to descend lower, all the more cracking and snapping his fingers. To the maiden said Frost:—

"Art thou warm, maiden? Art thou warm, fair one?"

The girl could scarcely draw her breath, but still she replied:

"Warm am I, Frost dear: warm am I, father dear!"

Frost began cracking more than ever, and more loudly did he snap his fingers, and to the maiden he said:—

"Art thou warm, maiden? Art thou warm, pretty one? Art thou warm, my darling?"

The girl was by this time numb with cold, and she could scarcely make herself heard as she replied:—

"Oh! quite warm, Frost dearest!"

Then Frost took pity on the girl, wrapped her up in furs, and warmed her with blankets.

Next morning the old woman said to her husband:—

"Drive out, old greybeard, and wake the young couple!"

The old man harnessed his horse and drove off. When he came to where his daughter was, he found she was alive and had got a good pelisse, a costly bridal veil, and a pannier with rich gifts. He stowed everything away on the sledge without saying a word, took his seat on it with his daughter, and drove back. They reached home, and the daughter fell at her stepmother's feet. The old woman was thunderstruck when she saw the girl alive, and the new pelisse and the basket of linen.

"Ah, you wretch!" she cries. "But you shan't trick me!"

Well, a little later the old woman says to her husband:—

"Take my daughters, too, to their bridegroom. The presents he's made are nothing to what he'll give them."

Well, early next morning the old woman gave her girls their breakfast, dressed them as befitted brides, and sent them off on their journey. In the same way as before the old man left the girls under the pine.

There the girls sat, and kept laughing and saying:

"Whatever is mother thinking of! All of a sudden to marry both of us off! As if there were no lads in our village, forsooth! Some rubbishy fellow may come, and goodness knows who he may be!"

The girls were wrapped up in pelisses, but for all that they felt the cold.

"I say, Prascovia! the frost's skinning me alive. Well, if our bridegroom doesn't come quick, we shall be frozen to death here!"

"Don't go talking nonsense, Mashka; as if suitors generally turned up in the forenoon. Why it's hardly dinner-time yet!"

"But I say, Prascovia! if only one comes, which of us will he take?"

"Not you, you stupid goose!"

"Then it will be you, I suppose!"

"Of course it will be me!"

"You, indeed! there now, have done talking stuff and treating people like fools!"

Meanwhile, Frost had numbed the girl's hands, so our damsels folded them under their dress, and then went on quarrelling as before.

"What, you fright! you sleepy-face! you abominable shrew! why, you don't know so much as how to begin weaving: and as to going on with it, you haven't an idea!"

"Aha, boaster! and what is it you know? Why, nothing at all except to go out to merry-makings and lick your lips there. We'll soon see which he'll take first!"

While the girls went on scolding like that, they began to freeze in downright earnest. Suddenly they both cried out at once:

"Whyever is he so long coming. Do you know, you've turned quite blue!"

Now, a good way off, Frost had begun cracking, snapping his fingers, and leaping from fir to fir. To the girls it sounded as if some one was coming.

"Listen, Prascovia! He's coming at last, and with bells, too!"

"Get along with you! I won't listen; my skin is peeling with cold."

"And yet you're still expecting to get married!"

Then they began blowing on their fingers.

Nearer and nearer came Frost. At length he appeared on the pine, above the heads of the girls, and said to them:

"Are ye warm, maidens? Are ye warm, pretty ones? Are ye warm, my darlings?"

"Oh, Frost, it's awfully cold! we're utterly perished! We're expecting a bridegroom, but the confounded fellow has disappeared."

Frost slid lower down the tree, cracked away more, snapped his fingers oftener than before.

"Are ye warm, maidens? Are ye warm, pretty ones?"

"Get along with you! Are you blind that you can't see our hands and feet are quite dead?"

Still lower descended Frost, still more put forth his might, and said:

"Are ye warm, maidens?"

"Into the bottomless pit with you! Out of sight, accursed one!" cried the girls—and became lifeless forms.

Next morning the old woman said to her husband:

"Old man, go and get the sledge harnessed; put an armful of hay in it, and take some sheep-skin wraps. I daresay the girls are half-dead with cold. There's a terrible frost outside! And, mind you, old greybeard, do it quickly!"

Before the old man could manage to get a bite he was out of doors and on his way. When he came to where his daughters were, he found them dead. So he lifted the girls on to the sledge, wrapped a blanket round them, and covered them up with a bark mat. The old woman saw him from afar, ran out to meet him, and called out ever so loud:

"Where are the girls?"

"In the sledge."

The old woman lifted the mat, undid the blanket, and found the girls both dead.

Then, like a thunderstorm, she broke out against her husband, abusing him saying:

"What have you done, you old wretch? You have destroyed my daughters, the children of my own flesh and blood, my never-enough-to-be-gazed-on seedlings, my beautiful berries! I will thrash you with the tongs; I will give it you with the stove-rake."

"That's enough, you old goose! You flattered yourself you were going to get riches, but your daughters were too stiff-necked. How was I to blame? it was you yourself would have it."

The old woman was in a rage at first, and used bad language; but afterwards she made it up with her stepdaughter, and they all lived together peaceably, and thrived, and bore no malice. A neighbor made an offer of marriage, the wedding was celebrated, and Marfa is now living happily. The old man frightens his grandchildren with (stories about) Frost, and doesn't let them have their own way.

# THE SOLDIER and DEATH

Once upon a time there was a soldier who had served God and the Great Sovereign for twenty-five whole years, and had only in the end earned three biscuits, and was journeying back home. And, as he went along, he thought: "Lord! here am I; I have served my Tsar for twenty-five years, have received my food and dress, and what have I lived for after all? I am cold and hungry, and have only three biscuits to eat." So he pondered and thought, and decided to desert and run away whither his eyes might lead him.

As he went along he met a poor beggar who asked alms of him. The soldier gave him one biscuit, and kept two. And, as he trudged on, he soon came across another poor beggar, who bowed down low and asked for alms. So the soldier gave him another biscuit, and had only one left. Again on he went, and met a third beggar. The old fellow bowed low and asked for alms. The soldier got his last biscuit out, and thought: "If I give him the whole, I shall have none left; if I give half, why, this old man will come across brother-beggars, will see they have a whole biscuit, and be offended. Better let him have it all, and I shall get on somehow." So he gave his last biscuit, and had nothing left.

Then the old man asked him: "Tell me, good man, what do you wish? Of what have you need? I will help you."

"God bless you!" the soldier answered. "How should I take anything of you?— you are old and poor."

"Don't think of my poverty," he replied. "Just say what you would like, and I will requite you according to your own goodness."

"I want nothing; but, if you have any cards, give me some as a keepsake."

For the old man was Christ Himself walking on earth in a beggar's guise. The old man put his hand into his breast and drew out a pack of cards, saying: "Take them. With whomsoever you play, you will win the game; and here you have a nosebag. Whatever you meet on the way, whether wild beast or bird that you would like to catch, just say to it: 'Jump in here, beast or bird!' and your wish will be carried out."

"Thank you!" said the soldier, took the cards and the nosebag, and fared forth.

He went on and on, may-be far, may-be near, may-be short, may-be long, and arrived at a lake, on which three wild geese were swimming. Then the soldier suddenly remembered the nosebag and thought: "I'll just test this nosebag"; took it out, opened it, and said: "Hi! you wild geese, fly into my nosebag!" No sooner uttered than the geese flew straight up from the lake into the bag. The soldier grabbed the bag, tied it up, and went on his way.

He travelled on and on and came to a town. He entered an eating-house and told the inn-keeper: "Take this goose and cook it for my supper, and I will give you another goose for your pains. Change me this third one for *vódka*." So there the soldier sat like a lord in the inn, at his ease, drinking wine and feasting on roast goose.

It occurred to him suddenly he might peer out of the window, and he saw opposite a big palace, but not one pane of glass was whole. "What is this?" he asked the inn-keeper. "What is this palace? Why does it stand empty?"

"Why, don't you know?" the master replied. "Our Tsar built himself this palace, but cannot inhabit it; and, for seven years, it has been standing empty. Some unholy power drives every one out of the place. Every night an assemblage of devils meets there, make a row, dance, play cards, and perpetrate every sort of vileness!"

So off the soldier went to the Tsar. "Your Imperial Majesty," quoth he, "please let me spend one night in your empty palace!"

"What do you mean, fellow?" said the Tsar. "God bless you; but there have been some dare-devils like you who passed a night in this palace, and not one emerged alive!"

"Well, still, a Russian soldier cannot drown in water, or burn in fire. I served God and the Great Sovereign five-and-twenty years, and never died of it; and, for one night's service for you, I am to die! No!"

"But I tell you: a man enters the palace at night alive, and only his bones are found there in the morning!"

But the soldier stood firm: he must be admitted into the palace.

"Well," said the Tsar, "go, and God help you. Stay the night there if you will; you are free, and I won't hinder you!"

So the soldier marched into the palace, and settled himself down in the biggest saloon, took his knapsack off and his sabre, put the knapsack in a corner and the sabre on a hand-peg, sat down on a chair, put his hand into his pocket for his tobacco-pouch, lit his pipe, and smoked at his ease. Then about midnight, I don't know where from, hordes of devils, seen and unseen, scurried up, and made such a turmoil and row, and set up a dance with wild music. "What, you here, discharged soldier!" all the devils began yelling. "Welcome! Will you play cards with us?"

"Certainly; here I have a set ready. Let's start!"

He took them out and dealt round. They began, played a game out, and the soldier won; another, and the same luck; and all the finessing of the devils availed them nothing; the soldier won all the money, and raked it all together.

"Stop, soldier," the devils said. "We still have sixty ounces of silver and forty of gold. We'll stake them on the last game." And they sent a little devil-boy to fetch the silver.

So a new game commenced; and then the little devil had to pry in every nook and come back and tell the old devil: "It's no use, grandfather—we have no more."

"Off you go; find some gold!" And the urchin went and hunted up gold from everywhere, turned an entire mine inside out and still found nothing: the soldier had played everything away.

The devils got angry at losing all their money, and began to assault the soldier, roaring out: "Smash him up, brothers! Eat him up!"

"We'll see who'll have the last word if it comes to eating," said the soldier, shook the nosebag open, and asked, "What is this?"

"A nosebag," said the devils.

"Well, in you all go, by God's own spell!" And he collected them all together—so many you couldn't count them all! Then the soldier buckled the bag tightly, hung it on a peg, and lay down to sleep.

In the morning the Tsar sent for all his folks. "Come up to me and inform me how does it stand with the soldier. If the unholy powers have destroyed him, bring me his little bones."

So off they went and entered the palace, and there saw the soldier trudging up and down gaily in the rooms and smoking his pipe. "Well, how are you, discharged soldier? We never expected to see you again alive. How did you pass the night? What kind of bargain did you make with the devils?"

"What devils! Just come and look what a lot of gold and silver I won off them. Look, what piles of it!" And the Tsar's servants looked and were amazed. And the soldier told them: "Bring me two smiths as fast as you can. Tell them to bring an iron anvil and a hammer."

Off they went helter-skelter to the smiths, and the matter was soon arranged.

The smiths arrived with iron anvil and with heavy hammers.

"Now," said the soldier, "take this nosebag and beat it hard after the ancient manner of smiths."

So the smiths took the nosebag, and they began to whisper to each other: "How fearfully heavy it is! The devil must be in it."

The devils shrieked in answer: "Yes, we are there, father—yes, we are there! Kinsmen, help us!"

So the smiths instantly laid the nosebag on the iron anvil, and they began to knock it about with their hammers as though they were hammering iron.

Very soon the devils saw that they could not possibly stand such treatment, and they began to shriek: "Mercy on us!—mercy on us! Let us out, discharged soldier, into the free world. Unto all eternity we will not forget you, and into this palace never a devil shall enter again. We will forbid everybody—all of them—and drive them all a hundred *versts* away."

So the soldier bade the smiths stop, and as soon as he unbuckled the nosebag the devils rushed out, and flew off, without looking, into the depths of hell—into the abysses of hell. But the soldier was no fool; and as they were flying out he laid hold of one old devil—laid hold of him tight by his paw. "Come along," he said; "give me some written undertaking that you will always serve me faithfully."

The unholy spirit wrote him out this undertaking in his own blood, gave it him, and took to his heels.

All the devils ran away into the burning pitch, and got away as fast as they could with all their infernal strength, both the old ones and the young ones; and henceforth they established guards all round the burning pit and issued stern ordinances that the gates be constantly guarded, in order that the soldier and the nosebag might never draw near.

The soldier came to the Tsar, and he told him some kind of tale how he had delivered the palace from the infernal visitation.

"Thank you," the Tsar answered. "Stay here and live with me. I will treat you as if you were my brother."

So the soldier went and stayed with the Tsar, and had a sufficiency of all things, simply rolled in riches, and he thought it was time he should marry. So he married, and one year later God gave him a son. Then this boy fell into such a fearful illness—so terrible that there was nobody who could cure it—and it was beyond the skill of the physicians; there was no understanding of it. The soldier then thought of the old devil and of the undertaking he had given him, and how it had run in the undertaking: "I shall serve you eternally as a faithful servant." And he thought and said: "What is my old devil doing?"

Suddenly the same old devil appeared in front of him and asked: "What does your worship desire?"

And the soldier answered: "My little boy is very ill. Do you know how to cure him?"

So the devil fumbled in his pocket, got out a glass, poured cold water into it, and put it over the head of the sick child, and told the soldier: "Come here, look into the water." And the soldier looked at the water; and the devil asked him: "Well, what do you see?"

"I see Death standing at my son's feet."

"Well, he is standing at his feet; then he will survive. If Death stands at his head, then he cannot live another day." So the devil took the glass with the water in it and poured it over the soldier's son, and in that same minute the son became well.

"Give me this glass," the soldier said, "and I shall never trouble you for anything more." And the devil presented him with the glass, and the soldier returned him the undertaking.

Then the soldier became an enchanter, and set about curing the boyárs and the generals. He would go and look at the glass, and instantly he knew who had to die and who should recover. Now, the Tsar himself became ill, and the soldier was called in. So he poured cold water into the glass, put it at the Tsar's head, and saw that Death was standing at the Tsar's head.

The soldier said: "Your Imperial Majesty, there is nobody in the world who can cure you. Death is standing at your head, and you have only three hours left of life."

When the Tsar heard this speech, he was furious with the soldier. "What, what!" he shrieked at him. "You who have cured so many *boyárs* and generals, cannot do anything for me! I shall instantly have you put to death."

So the soldier thought and thought what he should do. And he began to beseech Death. "O Death," he said, "give the Tsar my life and take me instead, for it doesn't matter to me whether I live or die; for it is better to die by my own death than to suffer such a cruel punishment."

And he looked in the glass, and saw that Death was standing at the Tsar's feet. Then the soldier took the water and sprinkled the Tsar, and he recovered completely. "Now, Death," said the soldier, "give me only three hours' interval in order that I may go home and say farewell to my wife and my son."

"Well, you may have three hours. Go," Death replied.

So the soldier went away home, lay down on his bed, and became very ill.

And when Death was standing very near him, she said, "Now, discharged soldier, say good-bye quickly—you have only three minutes left to live in the bright world."

So the soldier stretched himself out, took his nosebag from under his head, opened it, and asked: "What is this?"

Death answered: "A nosebag."

"Well, if it is a nosebag, then jump into it!"

And Death instantly jumped straight into the bag. And the soldier, ill as he was, jumped up from his bed, buckled the nosebag together firmly, very tightly, threw it on his shoulder, and went into the Bryánski Woods, the slumbrous forest. And he went there, and he hung this bag on the bitter aspen, on the very top twig, and he went back home.

From that day forward nobody died in that kingdom: they were born, and they kept on being born, and they never died. And very many years went by, and the soldier never took his nosebag down. One day he happened to go into the town. He went, and on his way he met such an old, old lady, so old that on whichever side the wind blew, she inclined. "Oh, what an old lady!" the soldier said. "Why, it is almost time she died."

"Yes, father," the old dame replied. "The time has come and gone long since. At the time when you put Death into the nosebag I had only one hour left in which to live in the white world. I should be very glad to have some rest; but unless I die, earth will not take me up; and you, discharged soldier, are guilty of an unforgivable sin in God's eyes. For there is no single soul left on earth who is tortured as I am."

Then the soldier stayed and began to think. "Yes, yes; it would be better to let Death out; perhaps I, too, might die. And beyond this, too, I have many sins on my conscience. Thus it is better now whilst I am still strong and I bear pain on this earth; for when I shall become very old then it will be all the worse for me to suffer anything."

So he got up and he went up into the Bryánski Woods, and he went up to the aspen, and saw there the nosebag was hanging very high, shaking in the winds to all sides. "Oh, you Death," he says, "are you still alive?"

A faint voice came out of the nosebag: "Yes, father, I am alive."

So the soldier took the nosebag, opened it, and he let out Death.

And he himself lay down on his bed, bade farewell to his wife and son, and he begged Death that he might die. And she[1] ran outside the door with all the strength in her feet. "Go!" she cried. "It is the devils who shall slay you—I shall not slay you!"

So the soldier remained alive and healthy. And he thought: "Shall I go straight into the burning pitch, for then the devils will throw me into the seething sulphur until such time as my sins shall have been melted from off me." And he bade farewell from all, and he went with the knapsack in his hand straight into the burning pitch.

And he went on: may-be near, may-be far, may-be downhill, may-be uphill, may-be short, may-be long; and he at last arrived in the abyss, and he looked, and all round the burning cauldron there stood watchmen. As soon as he stopped at the gate a devil asked who was coming.

"A guilty soul to be tortured."

"Why do you come? What are you carrying with you?"

"Oh, a nosebag."

And the devil shrieked out of his full throat and made a tremendous stir. All the infernal powers roused themselves and looked out of the gates and windows with their unbreakable bolts.

And the soldier went all round the cauldron, and he called out to the master of the cauldron: "Let me in, please; do let me into the cauldron. I have come to you to be tortured for my sins."

"No, I will not let you in. Go away wherever you will—there is no room for you here."

"Well, if you will not let me in to be tortured, at least give me two hundred souls. I will take them up to God, and perhaps the Lord will pardon my faults."

And the master of the cauldron answered: "I will add fifty more souls to the lot; only do go away!" So he instantly ordered two hundred and fifty souls to be counted out and to be taken to the rear gates in order that the soldier might not see him.

---

1. Death is feminine in Russian.

So the soldier gathered up the guilty souls, and he went up to the gates of Paradise.

The Apostles saw him, and said to the Lord: "Some soldier or other has come up here with two hundred and fifty souls from hell!"

"Take them into Paradise, but do not let the soldier in."

But the soldier had given up his nosebag to one guilty soul, and had told it: "Just look here. When you enter the gates of Paradise, say at once: 'Soldier, jump into the nosebag!'"

Then the gates of Paradise opened, and the souls began to go in; and this guilty soul also went in, and for sheer joy forgot all about the soldier.

Thus the soldier was left behind, and could not find any home in either place, and for long after that he still had to live and go on living in the white world. And after very many days he died.

# A NOTE ON THE SOURCES

The stories in this book were collected, translated, and published in the late nineteenth and early twentieth centuries. They have been excerpted from the following publications, all of which are in the public domain.

Curtin, Jeremiah. *Myths and Folk-Tales of the Russians, Western Slavs, and Magyars.* Boston: Little, Brown, and Company, 1903. Translated from the original of Alexander Afanasyev (1890). https://archive.org/details/mythsandfolktal00curtgoog/page/n14/mode/2up

Magnus, Leonard A. *Russian Folk-Tales.* London: Kegan Paul, Trench, Trubner and Co., and New York: E. P. Dutton and Co., 1915. Translated from the original by Alexander Afanasyev. https://archive.org/details/russianfolktales00afan_0/page/n5/mode/2up

Naaké, John Theophilus. *Slavonic Fairy Tales.* London: Henry S. King and Co., 1874. Translated from the originals of M. Maksimovich, B. Bronnitsuin, and E. A. Chudinsky https://archive.org/details/slavonicfairyta00naakgoog/page/n9/mode/2up

Shedden-Ralston, William Ralston. *Russian Fairy Tales.* New York: Pollard and Moss, 1887. Translated from the originals of Alexander Afanasyev, Ivan Khudyakov, A. A. Erlenvein, and E. A. Chudinsky. https://archive.org/details/russianfairytale00rals/page/10/mode/2up

# SOURCES

**The Baba Yaga**
From *Russian Fairy Tales* by William Ralston Shedden-Ralston

**The Book of Magic**
From *Slavonic Fairy Tales* by John Theophilus Naaké

**Frost**
From *Russian Fairy Tales* by William Ralston Shedden-Ralston

**Go to the Verge of Destruction and Bring Back Shmat-Razum**
From *Myths and Folk-Tales of the Russians, Western Slavs, and Magyars* by
Jeremiah Curtin

**Ivan the Peasant's Son and the Little Man Himself One-Finger Tall, His Mustache Seven Versts in Length**
From *Myths and Folk-Tales of the Russians, Western Slavs, and Magyars* by
Jeremiah Curtin

**Ivan Tsarevich, the Fire-Bird, and the Gray Wolf**
From *Myths and Folk-Tales of the Russians, Western Slavs, and Magyars* by
Jeremiah Curtin

**Marya Morevna**
From *Russian Fairy Tales* by William Ralston Shedden-Ralston

**The Ring with Twelve Screws**
From *Myths and Folk-Tales of the Russians, Western Slavs, and Magyars* by
Jeremiah Curtin

**The Seven Simeons, Full Brothers**
From *Myths and Folk-Tales of the Russians, Western Slavs, and Magyars* by
Jeremiah Curtin

**The Smith and the Demon**
From *Russian Fairy Tales* by William Ralston Shedden-Ralston